Gaiety

SHORT STORIES

Peter Abbot

Rock's Mills Press
Rock's Mills, Ontario • Oakville, Ontario
2022

Published by
Rock's Mills Press
www.rocksmillspress.com

Contents

Toad and Frog

Toad and Frog were sitting on a bench.

The sun was shining. Birds were singing. It was a warm morning in Spring.

"What a beautiful day! Are you happy, Frog?" said Toad.

"Yes, I am happy" replied Frog. "Are *you* happy, Toad?"

"Yes, I am happy, Frog. But –" Toad put an arm around Frog, and hugged him. "I could be happier, Frog. And so could you."

"Happier?" asked Frog. "How could we be happier, Toad?"

"If you would love me, Frog."

"We have been best friends for many years, Toad."

"But I want more than friendship, Frog. I want –" And he kissed Frog.

Frog stood up. "No, Toad, I don't think that is possible!"

"But why, Frog? Why do you say it is not possible?" cried Toad.

"Because the children who hear our stories would not like it," said Frog. "And the parents who read our stories to their children would not buy our books. We must always stay as we are, Toad. We must stay best friends."

"We can *still* be best friends, Frog" said Toad. "We can even be *better* best friends, Frog, if we live together, and love each other." He stood up, and hugged Frog again, and held him very tight, and kissed him again. "Please, Frog, let's try."

Frog thought hard. He looked at the beautiful countryside. He heard the birds singing. He saw the flowers and new leaves. Then he smiled. "Yes, all right, Toad, let's try. Your Hole or mine?"

Toad smiled.

With affectionate acknowledgment of Frog **and** Toad are Friends *(Harper & Row, 1970), a children's book by Arnold Lobel.*

Maybe, Stellar, Perhaps

With a careful push from his father, Will wobbled off, gathered speed on the hill, swept round the first corner with aplomb, took the next one too fast, and crashed. He lay there for a moment, on his back, with the bike between his legs; deciding whether he was hurt, whether to cry.

Cal had run ahead of James; he reached Will just as he began to whimper; caught him up in strong arms, held him tight, and kissed him.

James reached them, puffing, and threw his arms round them. After a moment, "Oh, Buddy – you did so well! You're *riding*! On your own. You know how to balance now! Awesome! No more 'Maybe I'll be able to ride on my own next time'! Soon you'll be riding everywhere you want! What a guy!"

"Yes, you're great, Will, know that?" Cal laughed. He set Will down and bent to pick up the bike. "I bet you were still thinking 'Maybe this time', and then suddenly you're flying, flying, *flying*! Hey, you won't need a broomstick to get around the neighbourhood tonight!"

Will rubbed his eyes. "Cowboys don't ride broomsticks, they ride horses," he said.

"What a glorious day, it'll be a great evening! – best Halloween weather I can remember. Best Fall ever, best colours ever – look at that red maple!" They were driving back to James's apartment, Will's bike stowed in the back of James's green Ford Escape.

"I'm so glad you could take some time off from the studio, Cal" James said. "We had a great time, didn't we, Will? Even apart from your awesome ride!"

"Thank you, Uncle Cal."

"It was truly awesome, Will! Maybe soon I won't be just 'Uncle Cal' –"

"No, don't say that, Cal" interrupted James softly. "There's a ways to go, and who knows, maybe problems ahead."

"Problems? More problems?"

"I'll tell you later. Are we going for ice-creams, Will?"

"Oh yes – please, Dad! Uncle Cal, it's close by Dad's new place. Maybe you know it? Best ice-creams ever!"

"No, but I guess I'm going to! Maybe we'll be going there often? But today's special, isn't it? A day of triumph! I want to take a photo of you and your Dad together, licking each other's ice-creams – and noses."

"He'll soon be asleep now, Cal. Couple of pages of his favourite *Curious George* and his eyes were closing. Listen – silence! I hope you helped yourself to a beer? Good. When he's had a very active day, and feels successful and happy, and all warm after his bath –"

"It's your low, warm voice, James, that does it. Sexiest voice on television, my Producer says so, and if *she* says so – ! But what's happening? Why so edgy? Aren't you going to come and sit next to me?"

"Of course. Let me get my beer. And heat up the pizzas. And maybe then I'll kiss you as a reward for your patience. Maybe."

"Oh yes – please. I'm waiting. And maybe after that – ?"

"Yes, yes, yes. Definitely. No 'maybe' about it! Look, I'm ready for you. Will you stay the night?"

"Please. But you'll have to wake me up so's I can be gone before Will wakes up, if that's still part of the deal – I'm not good at getting up in the middle of the night, as you must have noticed! Especially after making love with you, Sire. Talk about exhaustion! Strange not to be in Toronto tonight – have you ever done Church Street at Hallowe'en? Not what it was, they say, but still a lot of scary fun. Those Queens! I always enjoyed all that. Last year I missed it because of the Australian trip. And now – But it was great fun shadowing you two round the neighbourhood and watching Will trick-or-treating in his cowboy outfit – 'Your money or your Candy!' – Even if I had to pretend I was just a passer-by."

"Well, we'll have to make up for that. Here. Put that beer down while I kiss you. Mmm. Yup, that's a start. And the pizzas will be ready soon. And after that –"

After that, they showered together, enjoyed almost-silent sex ("Sh, sh – I think I can hear him stirring"), and lay side by side on James's capacious bed.

"You asked if it's still important that we don't act like lovers in front of Will" James said softly. "Yes it is, Cal. I'm sorry, but – See, it's still touch-and-go with Julie. I'm sure she interrogates him after every weekend with me. As I told you, the judge gave me alternate weekends, and other occasional access, like birthdays. Julie was angry about that. You know she accused me of sexually molesting Will – I couldn't believe it! But, thank goodness, the judge didn't seem to believe it either."

"That's shocking, James. How can they go on equating homosexuality with pedophilia? Seems we still have a ways to go."

"And she sent me an e-mail recently telling me that she and her boyfriend – his name's Brandon, he's also from Winnipeg, she said, an old high-school friend, works in a bar on Locke now – and she said they want to have Will permanently – for *his* sake, of course. 'He's my son, I love him, and I don't want him confused and messed up about who he is, he needs to be in a family' etcetera etcetera. I replied that I love him too, I'm his father, and he needs both his parents to develop a secure identity. But I can see she doesn't accept the situation – she's always abrupt with me when I pick Will up, often keeps me waiting, makes a fuss about his clothes, lectures me about food and says I let him get cold, etcetera. I really think she'd go back to her lawyer if I gave her half a chance, and they'd try to push me out of Will's life altogether. That's what worries me."

"I'm sorry, James. He's a great kid, and he loves you, anyone can see that. It's been so good to get to know him today. Why is she so angry – Julie? Just because you found you're gay?"

"He loves you too, Cal. Oh, if only Julie would lighten up – Yup, I guess it's mainly because I'm gay. Of course I can understand her anger to some extent, and even sympathise with it, as I told you – her disappointment, and that she feels betrayed by me. And her family, her parents and her brother, they're very religious – I remember Julie saying they were all furious that same-sex marriage is legal now in Canada, their Church fought against that – So, well, you know how it is – for them, I'm the ultimate Sinner – they wouldn't even talk to me after she told them I was gay and she was getting a divorce. See – I decided I had to level with her, couldn't go on living a lie – well, I told you about all that, didn't I? Yes, I did suspect I was gay when we married, so, yes, I *was* dishonest, I guess, and didn't keep my marriage vows – she accused me of that – But when we married I was convinced I could change, and I did manage in bed with Julie for a while, otherwise how did we produce Will? But – oh, Cal, increasingly I longed for sex with men, and especially a loving relationship with a man – and then I met you, and you and I – Was it only three months ago? You know how much I love you, Cal. That I want to be with you for as long as we live?"

"Yes. And you know I love *you*, James. But hey, it wasn't just three months ago – that was when you broke your silence and we talked – but we already knew each other pretty well, or I knew you – through working together on that show – Maybe I never told you this, but I did wonder even then if maybe you were gay – my gaydar, you know – but I also knew you were married with a child – so I kept my distance. Hey, is this Confession Time all over again? But with Will – does it have to be 'Uncle Cal' – always 'Uncle Cal'? Then he'll find it hard later to ever call me Dad. And will I always have to pretend not to be with the two of you when we're not inside your apartment or your car? Even when you and I move in together? I hope not. Actually I felt a bit embarrassed and awkward tagging along behind you this evening. Will looked so great, and so happy, in his cowboy costume, and you too, so proud and happy, holding his hand while the neighbours gave him compliments and candy – and there was I, lurking in the shadows, trying to look disconnected from you, hoping no-one would report seeing a pedophile in the neighbourhood!

– I guess I also felt a bit humiliated. Like you, I want to be honest and open about our relationship. For Will's sake too."

"I hope it won't be for long now, Cal. I think Julie'll come round after a while – if her relationship with Brandon lasts, and I even wonder if she's pregnant now, she's putting on weight, maybe she was even pregnant before the divorce. And with another child maybe she'll relax some. But it's going to be tricky, Cal. It's tricky now, and will be for a while longer. You can see that. I'd hate for you to get drawn into any of my problems, any anger between Julie and me. I'd rather you leave me if that happens. Last thing I want is to mess up your life."

"Well, I won't be doing that. Leave you? Never! Here, turn you head, look at me, let me kiss you."

"But I don't think you noticed the car that parked near us this afternoon, other side of *my* car. The guy in it was watching us. I'm sure of it. And I thought –"

"Oh, I think you must have imagined that, James. We should avoid getting paranoid, don't you think? I guess we'll just have to live our lives and enjoy being together, and enjoy being with Will, and just ignore any nastiness anyone throws at us. So far so good! And maybe we'll soon be able to look back at where we are now, and smile about it. Hey, and I must get some sleep or I'll be a total wreck tomorrow. And I have to argue with Doug for the new format. So goodnight, Sire!" He kissed James on the neck, and flung an arm around him.

Cal called James early one morning, several weeks later. "Hi. I'm back!"

"Oh, Cal, I'm so glad! I was worried that you wouldn't make it before this big snowstorm came in."

"Got in last night just ahead of it. Bumpy flight, and it started snowing hard when I was in the taxi, and getting real bad by the time we reached my condo, and now the streets and sidewalks are a mess. How about you? Same in Hamilton, I guess?"

"When am I going to see you? All I've been doing is interviews with guys who lost a bundle in the Global Meltdown, and a story about Afghanistan and why we should get out of there before more of our guys are killed. And so on. Can't tell you how much I've been missing you! What's New York got that I haven't got? But thanks for all those emails, Cal, you know how I appreciate them – but it's *you* I want, it's *you* I need."

"And I can't wait to get my arms around you, James! I'm free this evening, once I've got things moving in the office. So how about I come over at say around eight?"

"Great! And I've got something to tell you."

"Something happen? How's Will?"

"He's fine. You can talk to him. He's just finishing his breakfast, then I'm taking him to school. He'll want to say a quick Hi. He's with me for two or three days, my Mom's coming over to look after him later, when I have to go in to the studio this afternoon. See – Julie's in Winnipeg, her Father's just been diagnosed with cancer, he's in hospital. Anyway, here's Will."

"Hi, Uncle Cal."

"Hi, Will. You good?"

"Yeah, I'm stellar. You coming to see us?"

"Tonight. I'll be coming over tonight. So hold your horses, pardner!"

" Stellar! Here's Dad."

"So we'll be seeing you later, Cal. Can you put Will to bed, and read to him? My Mom will have to get home to make supper for my Dad, so she'll be very glad to see you. She doesn't know about you and me yet – you know, that we're lovers – but you remember her, I introduced you to her at my Thanksgiving party, and she knows we're friends and colleagues. Can you do that? Sorry to bother you. I should be back before ten. Please be careful on the highway – there's been a whole lot of fender-benders and a few serious accidents, you know what it's like with the first snowstorm of the winter. You ready, Will?"

"Oh, no bother, James. I'll drive carefully, don't worry – I want to be at my best for you tonight – no bruises, no broken bones! And it'll be a pleasure to spend some time with Will – he's great company. But what's this 'stellar'?"

"Just the latest word of 'fulsome' approval. He's trying it out – replaces 'awesome', which replaced 'cool' – and it'll probably be replaced itself by 'stunning' or even 'fabulous' by tomorrow, who knows? Comes from his friend Andy, I think, who got it from his father. Maybe."

"'Maybe'. How about we replace *that* word, you and me? See you later, James. Perhaps."

"'*Perhaps*'? Did you say 'Perhaps'?"

"What? Oh, I didn't mean about this evening – Just joking! Don't worry, James, I'll definitely come over and see to Will. No problem! *You* drive carefully, Sire! See you later."

When James got home at around eleven, they sat on the floor in front of the fire that Cal had made; and, in a companionable silence, relished the remnants of a vegetable stew Cal had cooked for Will, washing it down with their favourite beer.

"So" Cal started. "What's doing? You've been silent about the home front for nearly a week and something tells me –"

"Yup, you're right. Two things, actually. Please don't be angry with me."

"Well" – Cal belched, threw two small logs on the fire. "Out with it, my man. What?"

"Out of chronological order. Apparently Julie deceived me – or half-deceived me. The trip to visit her sick father in Winnipeg was also to have an abortion. She called last night to say that she had to stay longer with her father because he's in very bad shape. What she didn't know was that Brandon, her boyfriend, now ex-boyfriend, had called me just before. He was drunk, and beside himself with fury, 'the fucking bitch', etcetera, 'it's *my* child, not just hers, she never even told me – never even fucking told me she was pregnant' – Apparently one of his sister's a nurse, and she happens to work for the abortion outfit that Julie booked into, and she recognised Julie, and called Brandon, and he tried to contact Julie, but it was too late. He called her mother and she didn't even know Julie was in Winnipeg."

"What a mess."

"Yup. That's for sure. I actually feel sorry for Julie, though of course what she did is wrong. But I wasn't really surprised because she had said a few times that one kid was enough, more than enough – she wasn't going to be trapped again at home looking after kids."

"You can't do anything about it, James. None of it's your fault. You're much too damn kind-hearted, truly you are. And *she* divorced *you*!"

"I know. But now Brandon has dumped her. Told me he loathes her, will have nothing more to do with her, 'You can have her back', and I think he means it. So what will Julie do? Well, I know her well enough to guess, and I'm worried. Not about her financial state – she's got a good job in a lawyer's office, and she got our house and furniture –"

"Because you were too kind to fight her –"

" – but her psychological state. She'll lash out, she always did if she was unhappy. And that's where the other thing comes in. Please don't be upset, Cal. I know you'll think I should have told you at the time, but I didn't want – Remember I said I would hate for you to be hurt – And I know you must be fed up with all these complications and problems, and maybe they won't stop."

"So what is it, James? Out with it, out with it. It can't be that bad!"

"Well. You remember that day we took Will to the park – when he was learning to ride his bike? And he crashed, and you –"

"Yes. I picked him up."

"And kissed him. And how I said I thought there was someone watching, and a car parked nearby. Well, there *was* someone, and not only watching but taking photos. With his smart-phone."

"So – ?"

"So, the next day Julie calls and complains that one of Will's knees was bruised and one of his arms scratched, and his pants were dirtied and his shoes scuffed, when I returned him, and, worst of all, I allowed a strange man to kiss him and she has photos to prove it. Of course I explained what had happened, said you were a friend and just comforting Will because he was upset – not *hurt*, I said, just upset. And she says I must remember that she has evidence now that I'm not an adequate father, and I allow pedophiles access to Will."

"Oh, James, what bullshit! What sort of woman is she? Well, obviously the sort who aborts a child if she thinks it might inconvenience her. I'm glad I don't know her, have to make excuses for her. Who was the photographer, by the way?"

"Brandon. He said, if I wanted them, I could have the fucking photos too –"

"Oh, much too much too much too much, James!" Cal started laughing, turned and seized James, who laughed too as Cal tickled him, and they rolled over each other, punching and kissing wildly, until they were both breathless.

"We'll wake up Will" James gasped.

Later, sitting on the couch side by side, they drank coffee, then held each other.

"So what will I do, Cal? About Julie, I mean, and Will?"

"My dear James, it is much too late to do anything except go to bed. You have sinned unforgivably and I must leave you. But only after one final night together – for I must have my way with you once more before we part forever – Then I shall mount my horse and ride into the dawn. And maybe –" His lips clamped on James's for a long kiss. Then he drew back and gazed into James's eyes. "Perhaps –"

Our Fathers

From: Susan Browning <SusieB3@humail.com>
Sent: September 7, 2007 18:54 PM
To: Margery Browning <mdbrowning@univemail.ca>
Subject: Dad

Hi, Margy:

Hows it goin. Parties, parties, parties??? Hope U having fun, sisterdear, thats what univeritys for, hey. In th first wk anyways. I bet you think its BORING back here in Dundas without u BUT. Its NOT!!! Actaly Im woried, so that why im Emailing you. I know you got othr things to do & littlesister isnt top of the list rite now. But this not about me. Leastways not only about me, but also Mom and even U.

What hapened is THIS. Cos U and Mom both away (how was the drive by the way) & Dad too I was lonsome, my new class is a BUST th teacher is FOUL & my frends Carol an Autum (you know her, the fat one) not alowed to hang out at nite here on acount of Mom an Dad both bein away – & I knew Mom will be back soon, after she finishd helping Gromma move into home fr senyers – but cos of that feeling lonesome I desided to visit Dad at the Cotage for last wekend & not tell him frist, make it a suprize for his birthday. So I went by bus an walked th last bit which made me get to the Cotage later than I sxpectd, it was just geting dark.

I know Ull say I was STUPID an I guess I was. Mom wuold say that too & if she called home and no reply shed be woried but shes home now and she dident call so that was lucky. I dident tell her what hapened & she talking & talking so much abt Gromma I don think she thot about wht I did wile she ws away. But maybe I SHOUD tell her??? What yuo think? What this Email about.

So I say I got to th at about nine on Friday night. I saw lights on so I new Dad was ther, the door wsnt lockd so I jst walkd in, an I dident say anythng, cos of wantng to suprize him. I put down my backpack quitely an got out his present. Then I heard that th shower was runin whch ws suprizin, at that time of nite I mean, an as I came to th bathroom door the shower was switchd off. So I stood there watng fr Dad to com out. Sudenly the door opend and a NAKID BLACK MAN coms out, I nearly screemd I got sch a frite!!!!! He just stands ther wen he seen me, an I stand ther, an I don't know where to look, hes realy well built!! an a big dick swinging betwen his legs, an hes smilin an then he calls out Hey, Ronnyboy, you better come out here, an he says to me I guess you one of hs daughtrs, Im Leo, glad to meet ya and he steps forwrad an shakes my hand!!! Then Dad comes out the bedroom, hes got a towel round him, thnk th LORD!!! and he jst looks at me all embarast an says Susan, what you doing here you know I'm finishn my book an I say Happy Birthday Dad an I give him the present & he says Oh Thank you & the gy, Leo is his name, he laffs an says Come on, Ronny, ya got to open it so Dad does an then his towel drops down!! So I turn round and go into the kitchn and put water in the kettel and turn it on like Mom does if anythng hapens, like the time U u nearly drownd and the time I off of my bike an broke my arm. And Dad calls out Thank you Suse, its a great presnt (new golf shirt) and then he says We wll be out soon as dressd an have tea an suppr with you, have you had anythng to eat, look in the frige.

So I lay the table, and I find some cold sasages an cheese an bread an frute, and wile im doing tht I hear them wisperin and then they com, all clean an DRESSD, and we all sit down an drink tea and eat. Aftr a wile Dad clears hs throat like he does wen hes mad with us, abd he looks at Leo, an then he says Susan I got sumthng importnt to tell you and I wish I told you befor, sos you an Leo not embarst then he stops so I say What is it? an he says Susan you are very matur fr yr age (12) and I remembr yuo askd yr Mom an me about same sex marrage an all that last year and we talkd about that, an he stops agan an looks hard at Leo. So Thn Leo says Your Dad is gay, Susan, we are lovers, I came here to hav a holiday with him, Im going back to Detroyt tomorow.

An I lose it I burst into tears!!! Don't laff at me, Margy I coudlnt help it. They both of them sat ther lookin at me & I say to Dad You cant be gay, you are a marred man and a father. He gets up and comes to me and stands behind an masages my shoulders, you know how he dos that if you start cryin, an he says Susan Im so sory Ive upset you an Pepel an relashinships much mor complicatd youl find out one day an well talk about it tomorow but I say No now I want to talk about it now an Leo says Yes thats th best sos you can all u want to know an thn youll sleep good you must be very tird Il go for a wak now sos you an yur your father cn talk but I say I want hm to stay an tak with us (cos Dad gets kinda quite an besides I like th gy hes got a kind face hes a gentelman?).

So now we sit out on th patio in th dark an the mozzies not so bad just coupla bites an Dad an Leo anser my questns. How did it hapen? They met On line Dad says an chated, an he had a confernce in Winser so then they met an went to motel ther an liked each other a lot an made love (how do men make love do you know I dident ask them I was too embarast is it messng around an kissng like with men an woman and tuchng an also suckn ther cocks??). Then Leo says Your Dad an me, we realy love each other an we enjoy to be togethr like here an yr dad is a good man he loves you too but not the same way I love him an he loves me. I say does Mom know? Dad says Im going to tell her soons I get home. An then what will hapen, will u leave us like Unkel Phil left Anty Merl an Henry an Dian? Dad an Leo look at each othr an Leo says May be may be not, we got to work out lots frst. What about u I say, did you leave yur wife an childrn? One child Casy youl meet him tomorow whn he coms to drive me back to Detroyt he lives with me, his momma divorct me an marred anothr man cos Im gay like your fathr but I new I was gay befor I marred I wantd to hav chidrn an I thot Id change, your dad dident know he was gay till he met me or thats what he SEZ. An hes smiln at Dad an he says Susan its a grate privileg to meet you I nevr expectd to you a neat girl an I want to ask you a favor please don't tell your momma anythng about Yr Dady an me till he has spokn to her, they got to work it out see. I say yes I promis.

Margy, sory this is long i evn wondr if Email ths long wll work an if not u may nevr get it anyways!!! Now it's a hole week since Dad an me came home an I don think he has told Mom about bein gay an about Leo. Moms just th same she smiles an hums an sings in the kitchan. So what do I do. Dad looks at me sumtimes sort of puzzld and Id like to talk to him but i dont. And ther's sumthin else, I mean SUMONE ELSE! Frst I thot thers five of us got to work it out Mom an Dad an You an me an Leo but now thers SIX cos Casy came an we ar in love too Casy an me. Hes so FANTASTIC so goodlookin an cute an kind and FUNNY an his smile is a mile wide honest honest!!! an he plays th getar an sings like hiphop (17 yrs old). Wen he arivd drivin his fathers car (been to a rap consrt in Buffalo) in the aftrnoon Leo an Dad wer in bed I think doin it so I say to Casy Lets go fr a walk round th lake an so we did an he talked all abt th consrt an then he was singin an dancin to show me an we down by th lake an he says hey lets swim I got to cool down an i say We dont got bathn suits an if peple see what wll they think but he just gets nakid an jumps in an calls me an so I get nakid too an we swim an play an tuch each othr he tuches me down ther an I touch him hes got a big dick like his fathr (if U tell anybody else esp Mom I kill u!!!). Well thats all Im tellin U now anyways. Afterwrds we sit on our cloths an dry off an he kises me an says he loves me an I sure love him. An we give each othr our Email adreses an telifone numbrs an promis to get togethr agan soonest.

We wak slowly to th Cotage his arm is over my shouldr an we stop an kis and kiss an whn we in the Cotage cottage I hear the shower goin agan!!! but this time its Dad an when he coms out hes wearn hs towl Im waitn to hav a pee. Then Dad an Leo come out onto th deck an both dressd an Leo has a sootcase an he hugs Casy an says I hope its not coke I thnk Im smelln Son, I bettr drive an U can tell me all about the rap consrt to keep me awak we bettr get goin or well get back late an I gotta work early shift tomorow. He says goodby to me and kises my hand, then he an Dad hold each othr tite so tite an just look an look into each othrs eys VERY ROMENTICK!!! an nothin mor to say they musta said it all in the bedroom.

An thats it, Margy. THATS IT! I told you almost evrthing are you BORED??? Dad an me I think Im goin mad an I think he is too. I wish hed tell Mom an then wed get to work things out but shes hummin an Singin an he looks at me like helplss an I think about Leo an esp Casy an its like they R gettin smallr an smallr an I am too. So what can I do? Sumtimes i think Ill tell Mom sos we can start Workin things out, sumtimes I think I bettr not an ask Dad. What DO U THINK?

I hope your keepn fit an happy, dear BigSister. With my love (som of it!!!), Susie

Sleeping Beauty

–Well, look, dearie – if you want to be my partner, you just have to occasionally "put up with shit", as you so gracefully express it –

–Yes, I *know* you don't like to be called "dearie". But you *are* dear to me, Hugh, very dear, surely you know that?

–Yes, and I *know* "put up with shit" is a "*common* expression" – but don't you see, that's why it's objectionable – because it *is* common. "Common as dirt" is also a common expression, especially where *you* are, isn't it, dearie? Queen's English?

–Oh, and all right – you don't like "partner". Yes, I remember you said so. But, look, dearie, that's also a common expression, the only one I can think of, I mean the only almost non-judgmental one, to define two people of whatever gender who live together, or want to – eat and drink together, fuck together, talk to each other, love each other. And I *do* love you, my wild English rose, you know I do. I love your good taste, I love your voice, I love your clothes, all the little social and dare I say *sexual* tricks your English public-school education taught you – I love *all* of you, dearie – oh and *especially* your posh accent –

–No, I wasn't with her, why would you think that? What would I do with her – in the middle of the night I mean? I'm not *that* bi, dearie.

–Yes, but she's my *dancing* partner and that's *so* different from my everything-else partner, surely you understand that. Marcia's a *ballerina,* dearie. So it's a *professional* relationship. And, as I have just said, I *wasn't* with her when you called this morning. And I'm not with her now. She doesn't even *want* me to be with her when we're not working together, why would she, she's got a boyfriend, an older man, very boring, very rich –

–Yes, even older than me! – thank you so *very* much, dearie – We're *all* getting older, aren't we. And I'm *not* rich, whatever you think, just generous. And he *cherishes* her, you know, like I cherish you – when we're together, but *when* will that be – when, when,

when? You said you'd be at my premiere, you said you would *definitely* be here for me last night, "Oh *of course* I'll be there for you, how could I miss *that*" – That's what you said, remember?

–Yes, I know you were trying to be funny, and anyhow ageing doesn't bother me at all –

–Well, couldn't you leave her for even a few days? Is she *that* sick? I must say I notice that her sickness seems to increase just in time to keep you at home clucking round her when you have *promised* to be here with me -

–All right, I'm repeating myself, that's what you make me do – and I'll repeat myself if I want to *anyhow*, dearie, do you think *you* don't repeat yourself? Endlessly, sometimes. And all right, I won't say anything hurtful about your mother, in fact I won't even *mention* her again if it's such a delicate topic. But I do know how you feel, *I* loved *my* mother deeply too – if you'd met her you'd know what a lovely lady she was, how generous and understanding, she always encouraged me, how she always kept her promises, how she was always *there* for me, whatever the cost -

–Well, I know I've said it before, dearie, but only once or twice, *not* fifty times, and it's hard to know some of the time if you have actually *heard* what I say – and all I was going to say when you interrupted me is that I was always there for *my* mother too when she was sick, especially when she was dying of cancer – I stayed all night at the hospital when she was dying, I held her hand -

–The *point* of this is that I understand your love for your mother *if* she is as sick as you say – but also to say that *my* mother showed her love for me by cherishing me, being there for me, and never getting in the way of my other relationships –

–"Which were *many*", as you so rightly say, dearie, I was always a popular boy, even before I made it as "Canada's –

–Well, *thank you*, dearie. I thought you would never say anything about it, I thought you didn't really care whether last night was a success or not. And yes, it *was* – *fabulously* successful, ovations and flowers and all that, about twenty *standing* ovations, for both

Marcia and me, they *loved* us, wouldn't let us go. I was *exhausted*. And this morning's *Globe*'s review's title says it all: "Brilliant New Sleeping Beauty". And quite complimentary about me and also Marcia. Strelitzky, and you may recall I told you how sarcastic he can be, he said afterwards at the party "A triumph, my dollinks! You haf crowned my career!" and hugged us of course and actually *wept* on my shoulder –

–No, didn't I tell you, I'm sure I did, we never *actually* had a relationship, I'm not his type, not submissive enough, and anyhow he likes them blond *all over* –

–Yes, I *know* you called earlier, I heard your message, and I know you would have "asked me all about it in detail if I'd answered", and would have congratulated me *then*, but still I wondered, you took so long to do it *now*, as if other things like why I didn't answer were so very much more important. But thank you, it was *stunning*, that's what Eric said, a *stunning* success –

–And yes, you did leave me a "Good luck" message a few days ago, yes, "Break a leg" –

–*And* the flowers. Were lovely. *Lovely!* Marcia *adored* them.

–Yes, I was waiting for your to ask, I knew you *would* ask. I was with him last night, and this morning when you called, dearie. *He* is stunning too, Eric, just *stunning* – mid-twenties, tall, slim, red hair, you know how I go for that, he reminded me a bit of you, actually. Without the adorable accent. And ten years younger. *Superb* body, so – *lithe*, I told him he should have been a ballet-dancer like me, but he said he could never go through all the daily physical grind – he's a graduate student at U of T, you remember we walked round the colleges last summer – last time you were here, he's at Wycliffe College. Anyhow, he was in the line-up for me to sign programs after the performance last night, and before he got to me I knew *I* wanted to – get to know *him*, so I whispered to him to wait around for a few minutes, if he could – and he could. So –

–Well, I took him to the party, and it just went on from there.

–"Went where?" Well, here. He is *so* good in bed! You could learn a thing or two from him, dearie. Even I – I think *I* learned a thing or two from him. He's so – *inventive*. He called *me* a sleeping beauty and said he would wake me up, starting with a kiss – and *wow*, did I wake up! Did you know, Eric told me last night at the party – he's so *intelligent* too, and knowledgeable – that the original story of the Prince waking up the Princess from her deep sleep was even more erotic, he said – it wasn't a *kiss*, or not *just* a kiss, it was a *fuck*, he *fucked* her awake, and then she lived happily ever after –

–Eric? Well, I have a confession to make, dearie. He's right here – well, not *here* in bed with me at this very moment, he's in the shower, but he'll be back here in bed with me any moment, so you can talk to him if you like, then, and ask *him* any questions about his life and times. I told him about *you* after you called earlier, so you won't have to cover that.

–No? As you like. Oh, yes, and I *didn't* say I wasn't here when you called, dearie. I *was*. We were drinking champagne in bed, Eric and I. We listened to your message together, and he said it was so *sweet* of you to call, it was like an aphrodisiac – or did *I* say that? Then when you called again, this time, he listened in for a while, to our little conversation, then he got bored with it, when you were going on and on about your dying mother, so he went off to shower, but now – Oh yes – Yes, here he is, my erotic Eric, standing at the door and covering his nakedness with a towel – which I hope he will – Yes, oh my God, *yes* – I'll have to say goodbye, dearie.

–No, I think it's too late to talk about our relationship. I think it was probably *always* too late.

Hard Place

– Kevin? Hey, my friend, great to hear your voice. How goes?

– Well, I've got the best news for you, my friend – the very best, make you feel real good, I promise. Can you guess?

– No, that's not – no – It was in this morning's *Globe and Mail*, I just happened to see it.

– Yeah, well I'm – Hey, give me a chance, I was just gonna tell you. It's Sarton. He's dead. It says he was found by his cleaning-lady, in his bed. "Foul play not suspected", i.e. must be suicide –

– Yes, or heart-attack, or cancer, I guess so. Maybe. But then surely it woulda said, you know, "after suffering an apparent heart-attack" or "after a gallant fight with cancer", something like that, wouldn't it?

– Yeah, I agree, they shoulda told us soon as he died, but when have they ever done anything to help us? The police, the "authorities", whoever. Even just a short call –

– No, there's no more details, nothing new. Just he was a retired teacher and coach and he had been charged recently with acts of sexual abuse going back twenty years – that's what it says, I'm reading it right now, and it says the trial date had not been set.

– Kevin? You there?

– Yeah, I know it's a shock, it's unexpected, hey. But – Aren't you glad, doesn't it make you happy?

– Well, that he's gone – so's we won't have to see him any more. Won't have to be involved in the trial, see him standing there sneering while we answer his lawyer's trick questions, have to re-live it all – I promise you, *I'm* happy, Kevin. That fucking bastard. After what he did – Just, hey, just not needing to spend any time thinking about him, and having to know he's still around – hey, that makes me *real* happy.

– But why? I don't understand. Kevin?

– "*Closure*"? No, I don't believe in that – sorry. Closure just don't *happen*, that's what I think – not in this world. You know how I see it. Move on, move on, move on! You gotta move on. No looking back, no looking sideways – what's the point?

– But hey, not having to look at *him*, seeing – that face – looking at him in the court –

– "Making *him* look at *you*", Kev? Wouldn't do nothing for *me*, I promise you. Just start up all the bad memories again – you want that? *I* sure don't, Kevin. No, I don't.

– Well – so, we disagree about that, my friend, that's all it is – we disagree. Different personalities, hey – we always were. That's all. But won't make any difference to our friendship –

– Yeah, but now there's no choice, Kevin. He took that with him. No need to choose now.

– No, I mean, when he decided to go – and yeah, I *really* do think he committed suicide – he solved things for us too, hey. That's what I been saying – Now we don't even have to dread the trial, having to give evidence, all of that – Or *I* don't –

– No, Kevin. No. He *didn't* "win after all". He *lost*. And no, *not* because he was gay. What you mean? He was always a loser, he was a loser when he abused his authority as a teacher and coach, he was a loser when he – That's what Dave said, remember, and he was *right*, Kev, he was right. None of the garbage, any what he did to us, none of it was our fault, everybody said that. The guy was a loser.

– Well, that's a different thing, hey. Dave had more of it than we did – years of it, he really *really* suffered, we only had it for a year, and that was *because* of Dave – because he had the courage to *do* something, tell his mother, go to the police – Otherwise we –

– And remember what his mother said to us? At the funeral?

– Yeah, that's right, that Dave was *always* over-sensitive. She said she was always worried about him, even when he was a child – worried he would find the world a hard place, that's what she said, I remember her saying it, just like that, "a hard place". And, hey, it *is* a hard place, my friend. We found *that* out!

– No, I don't think – Yes, she *was* a kind person, but I don't think she was lying just so's we would respect what he did for us, be grateful.

– No. You remember Dave, we both do – always shy and quiet,

even though he was two years older than us – and that he hated violence –

– Kevin, yes I *do* remember what *you* said after the funeral – But you don't *really* envy Dave, I don't think so, you didn't really mean that, when you said you would follow him one day – You were just – Kevin, I don't think you –

– No, Kevin, no. Listen. *I* care. Let's get together, soon. *Soon*, hey?

– Because we're *friends*, my friend. Aren't we? Always friends, hey. We swore that. Remember? My closest friend. You know I care. And I want to catch up with your life, I want to know all about Vancouver, your life in Vancouver, I want to see Vancouver. And meet Jim – how's Jim doing? And we can – We can celebrate, even. We got so much to talk about, everything –

– Oh, I'm so sorry, Kev. Maybe he'll be back, maybe he just needed some time to –

– No, Kev, not your fault, it's *not* your fault, of course it's not. When relationships break up, it's both – two people make a relationship, hey – so both are responsible if it breaks up.

– Well, that's what I truly think, Kev. So, hey, how's about – you know, getting together? Maybe I can get coupla days off, sure I can, my boss is pretty decent – compassionate, he's a compassionate guy, you'd like him – So I'll come maybe even next weekend, how's about that?

– No, listen – Kev, I *will* come next weekend. *Definitely* next weekend. Whatever happens. Hey, Kev? Then we'll be able to –

– Kev? You there? Kev?

– Kev?

Very Special

Well, you don't expect it to last *forever*! Of course you don't. Nothing *does* (last forever, I mean). But I'm talking sex, here and now. And sex is about the shortest act in the firmament. Two minutes flat, from the moment of arousal to the moment of orgasm. Or shorter. I've timed it. Here and gone.

So that's what I told *him*. Later. He'd been looking at me, *gaping* at me, all night. But of course trying to look like he wasn't. Eventually (and I mean *eventually*) he stands up and comes across, *lurches* across. I was wishing I'd decided to go across to *him*, that would have been less embarrassing, I could have made it look like a washroom break. You see, I was with my two boyfriends – I call them that, it's a joke actually. They claim I'm a *slut*! That's a joke too, I think – but I do seem to be popular (especially with older men) – it's my personality, and my looks, and how I dress, I guess. One guy said I could be an Escort! I always try to look *special* – pink hair it was then, gold ear-rings, the pearly necklace, *tasteful* jewelry – and the scent too – just a touch, behind my ears, of that special perfume my favorite Daddy gave me on my seventeenth birthday.

Anyway. As I was saying – He lurched across. Of course I looked up, *so* surprised, and he said, deep dark voice (how I love that!) "Mind if I sit here?" and plopped down beside me before I could even reply.

Kyle's eyebrows were raised and Josh was grinning sideways. "Oh, now who might *you* be?" says Kyle, fluttering his eyelashes. "Another of Yolanda's *multitude* of admirers? Don't mind *us*. Josh and me can go and dance while you two get to know each other –"

"No, no," say I, "don't – no need to go – I don't know who –" turning to look hard at my new neighbor. "Who *are* you?"

And he smiles, shiny regular teeth, blue blue eyes, and I'm a *fool* for floppy black-hair little-boy style – and he holds out his right hand so's I have to take it in mine, though it was hard to reach over his muscular torso. "Lucien, *c'est moi.* Lucien, from Montreal" – his baritone, with that French accent, flowing smooth as honey. "I hope that I will know Torontonians – that is how you say it, yes? To-ron-tonians. And To-ronto."

You guessed it. We ended up in my bed, making wild, glorious,. *perfect* love. And in the morning, while I'm making us coffee and toast, he says "Yuri, Yuri – I love that your name is Yuri – I must return to Montreal this morning, *tout de suite*. Come! Accompany me. Tell me this address now, and I will communicate it on my cell-phone with the *chauffeur*, and he will pick us and transport us to Montreal. I wish to marry you, my Yuri, you will be my wife," and he leaned across the table and kissed me on my nose.

So what did I do? What would *you* have done? Well, I may be a slut, but I am not a *stupid* slut. He was rich (he drops that his father's a millionaire), and he's about thirty, my very *favorite* age, and he's *beautiful*, and he smells *so* good, and his *voice*, I wanted him to talk and talk, and he did, all the way to Montreal in the white stretched-limo. My *master*.

Yes, I say. Yes, yes please, to everything. And he has this gorgeous condo with a view over the St Lawrence – and *that afternoon* he took me to his Family's Factory (they manufacture pills) and introduced me to his Father, who murmurs how glad he is to make my connection, and his Mother, who smiles and holds out a perfumed hand for me to kiss and murmurs "*Enchantee*". Oh, I loved it all. All!

I knew it wouldn't last, of course. In fact, I could tell then that it was already ending. That's what I said when he came out the shower that night and held me in his dripping arms – I looked up at him and whispered "Lucien, this is a dream, it can't last, can it?" He kissed me and kissed me, and we made love, but he didn't answer, and he didn't mention marriage again. And actually, to be honest, I was already a touch bored. Just as well he had some E.

Next morning, while I'm waking up, he says "I must go to the office, *cherie*. In two hours I will return. Be at home, Yuri. Is that how you say it? Oh no – *Make yourself at home*, that is how you say it, yes? Make yourself at home."

I checked my cell-phone for messages and then accessed my

Emails on his computer. One from Josh, stupid stuff, he's with this hunk from Texas, and how Kyle was so fucking jealous he wouldn't talk to them!! One from my favorite Daddy, his name is Terence, "Where O where is my little Boyo???? Please cum to Daddy. Daddy has a little reward for a good little Boyo!!!!" (he always gives me a check for $500). And four from old guys responding to my Silver-Squirt Profile – two of them look worth checking out, for sure. Lonely rich geezers wanting a young guy to make them feel they're still alive. For a short while longer. Like I say, nothing lasts forever, and these four sure won't. But their money will.

So when Lucien got back, I was ready to move. Toronto, here I cum (back)! "Oh Lucien, I just had an urgent call from my Sister. My Mother had a very bad night, she's in hospital with cancer, she's asking for me."

"Oh, Yuri, sorry, sorry. I am so very sorry. Of course you must go to her, *tout de suite*. The *chauffeur* will drive you to the airport." He dialed a number on his cell-phone, and spoke rapidly (in French, of course). Then he comes to me and says, "Here, my Yuri –". The check he pulls from a pocket was already filled-in and signed.

"Oh, but this is too much, Lucien, much too much –"

"No, no, my Yuri, it is not *enough* – You are very special, Yuri. Keep in touch – that is how you say it, yes? Keep in touch. And when you will come to Montreal – Or when I will be in Toronto another time – We will –" He pulls me to him, hugs me, kisses me on the forehead. "Look after yourself, Yuri. You are very special."

So. Did all that happen? Yes, it did. I'm sure it did. Or did I imagine some of it? Four years ago, nearly. I haven't seen him since then – Lucien. And I haven't been back in Montreal. And I don't see Josh and Kyle now. Josh died, AIDS someone said, and Kyle went off somewhere, Australia, I think. And my favourite Daddy died, Terence, he gave me $2,000 the last time I saw him. But I have other Daddies. So. My Mom always said "Laugh and the world laughs with you" and that's true.

And So They Die

On a cool, rainy Spring morning, I stopped for a coffee in our local Koffee Kup. The Gang were there, already into their morning gossip. I call them the Gang because, although they smile pale Christian smiles at recognised faces, they are there to enjoy the company of their established companions and clearly would not welcome intrusion. (I should add that they're all members of a local church congregation – which I probably should not identify; and also that I am the recently-appointed Organist and Choir-master of another local church.)

When I sat down with my coffee, I could overhear their conversation, and began to listen deliberately when I heard one of the four elderly ladies, Jane, say "Yes, that was dreadful, a dreadful thing, truly dreadful. You didn't know about it, Iris? It was a shock to us all. He was the son of one of my friends in Dundas, and apparently he was gay, and he was attacked and beaten late one night. Apparently several men followed him and pushed right into his apartment before he could shut his door – he must have thought they were going to one of the other apartments. That was in the 'States somewhere, Texas I think. And do you know what the police said? 'Oh, those ones, they're always doing that to each other.' That's what I was told. And they've done nothing to try to catch them. And my friend's son was in hospital badly injured. She flew straight down to be with him, soon as she heard, but he died before she got there. It was in the *Spec*, about two weeks ago I think, one of the inside pages. I think Marlene is still down there. She's not a really *close* friend, we just chat together sometimes when we meet in the supermarket. I didn't know what to do."

"That could happen here. Well, in Toronto, for sure."

"Oh no, do you think so? No, in Canada we –"

"In Canada we're so much more tolerant? But if you go into some areas at night –"

"You mean in the gay village or whatever they call it in Toronto? Church Street?"

"Even in Hamilton, right outside here, you know at the lights – I was driving home late one night last week and this young girl, couldn't have been more than fifteen, she appears suddenly at my window when I stopped at the red – and she taps till I roll it down a bit, then she says 'Twenty dollars for the night', and I go 'Twenty, does that include breakfast?'"

"Oh Ernie, *no*, surely not. You wouldn't –"

"Well, not quite like that. I didn't say exactly that. But I wouldn't give her any money, that would have just encouraged what she was doing. Drugs, violence, prostitution, you don't think those sort of things happen here, but they sure do. They need money for drugs, and if they can't get it legally, and most of them got no job – that's how most youth get into crime. The police say that. Did you see the article about it in the *Spec*? She needed drugs, that girl, you could see it in her eyes, the way she stared. She was desperate."

I was watching Bruce. As Jane's story ended, he had tensed up. He sat frowning afterwards, tight-lipped, gripping the arms of his chair. But he said nothing. I know him slightly; as a fellow-organist, and he used to come occasionally to the meetings of a gay group I belonged to which was fighting for same-sex marriage – in the days before Parliament voted in favour, when we really thought the Bill might be defeated. One of the other organists I know, Guy, at St Christopher's, is a friend of his. But he's secretive, Bruce – like many gays. Like me.

By chance, when I came back from the washroom, he was leaving, saying goodbye to the Gang. I caught up with him on the sidewalk – "Hi, Bruce – how's it going?"

"Oh – Ed? I'm good. Yes – Integrity, wasn't it? Gay marriage. I remember we talked after one of those meetings."

"Can I walk with you? I was wondering – That was Geoff they were talking about?"

"Bitch! Those sweet old ladies, poison."

"But she wouldn't know that he and you –"

"Of course she would, they're always gossiping together. She looked at me whenever she mentioned him – as if what happened to him was somehow my fault. And so loud – like they want the world to hear. But that doesn't matter, I can deal with her if I have to. But it's so – I've been so upset about Geoff. I guess you didn't know him. He was in my Choir for two years, student at McMaster, best tenor I ever knew, untrained voice but you should have heard him – he could have had a career in opera – and he threw it all away –"

"After he graduated?"

"Wanted to do research, graduate work, something to do with Nuclear Medicine, apparently he was very good at whatever it was – but he was already into drugs and alcohol, long before I knew him. Parents divorced, dysfunctional family. In trouble with the law when he was a teenager. But he made an effort to get out of it. And I did everything I could to help him, while we were together, I really did. We – I loved him, I thought it would last. But then he left me for some sugar-daddy in Toronto. No warning of course, just walked out – and he lied to me – but I shouldn't – So now he's dead. What a waste. His mother – Well, I met her once or twice, she was a bitch – But she called me from Pennsylvania, asked me to come to his funeral, just last week – 'He loved being in your Choir, often talked about it when he was home.' But – You know, I couldn't afford it, and anyway can't just run off and miss Sunday services, and they're thinking about cutting the Choir, it's all about saving money – the budget, the budget – Same in your church?"

"Every church, I guess."

We had stopped at the corner, awkwardly. "Well, nice to have seen you, Bruce. I hope – all goes well – Have a good day."

"You too. Look after yourself."

So he didn't know that Geoff and I had been an item. After the "sugar-daddy in Toronto" had kicked him out. I met him in the local gay bar – a beautiful slim blond young guy, green eyes, sweet smile. Just four weeks together, last summer, that's all the time we had – four ecstatic weeks in the family cottage. *His* family's cottage. Yes, we did do some drugs. And he told me about having been with Bruce –

"Always going on about my voice, all he ever cared about – my voice, my voice, my voice." And he wouldn't sing for me at all.

When we got back to Hamilton and he announced he was leaving for the States – he hadn't told me anything about that earlier, and about having a scholarship at Penn State, only about being together with me for ever and ever – I was stunned, then angry. I said "Fuck off, then, and don't ever come back." Or words to that effect.

I can still see his smile, his two raised fingers. He said "Don't worry, Ed, I won't. Have a good life, buddy."

His mother called me too, couple of weeks back – that was the first I heard of it, his death. I'd met her once, when she came to the Cottage to collect his clothes for washing – we talked, and I think she liked me. And so *she* called me too, and, after telling me he'd been murdered, she said "You were one of his best friends, Ed, he told me he loved you."

But *I* didn't get to the funeral either.

Sin is Behovely

Bishop Michael Murnaghan is a burly, ruddy, jolly fellow.

"He wants to meet you," Piers told me. "You'll like him, even if you're not a member – yet – of the True Faith. He'd heard about you, of course. So when can you come? He suggests dinner tomorrow evening."

"As soon as that? He's a quick worker – or maybe he leaves all the work to you and the other priests?"

"Oh no. I think he just had an open evening. He loves having guests, anyway – he's very gregarious – though of course you're special."

"Really? In what way? Surely not just because I'm gay?"

"You'll find out. I won't say any more and spoil your first encounter with our deeply-loved lord and master."

So there I was, the next evening, Saturday, standing at the front-door of Bishops Mount, an impressively large, stone, secluded Victorian mansion whose interior, I was soon to observe, had been renovated extensively and tastefully into a domain of maximum comfort.

The first snow of winter was still falling softly when I rang the bell. I turned to look, through cavorting snowflakes and between black firs, at the fine view over the lake, mournfully beautiful in the soft, grey light of evening. As the chimes died away, the door opened silently, and a slim, handsome, dark-haired young man, in a red t-shirt, jeans and sandals, smiled at me. "Please come in, Mr McKnight. The Bishop is expecting you," he said, and led me into the entrance-hall – where I deposited my coat and shoes – and then into a large, high-ceilinged and deep-carpeted room, furnished opulently, and warmed by a leaping fire.

The young man went across to the imposing fireplace (was he a Priest in informal dress or a Brother? I wondered). While putting more logs on the fire and poking it into even greater activity, he said, over his shoulder, "Please sit down, Mr McKnight. The Bishop will not be long; unfortunately, he has had to take an unexpected phone-call from the Vatican."

"Are you his secretary?" I asked, as I sank into one of the plum-coloured couches.

"I'm Father Jeremy, the Bishop's Chaplain." He got up and came to me with his arm outstretched. "I apologize, I should have introduced myself earlier." We shook hands. "No, I'm not a secretary. Sister Alma comes over from the Convent every day; she's not only an excellent secretary but a ferociously dedicated housekeeper who keeps this place in strict order. She even cooks – claims she *loves* to cook. In fact, her main vocation seems to be to serve the Bishop, and Mother Superior seems to agree, thank God. One hopes both of them will be rewarded in Heaven. Now I'm afraid I must leave you – I have a sermon to finish for Mass tomorrow – but we'll meet again after dinner."

Left alone, I got up to examine the multitude of books neatly arranged in an imposing bookcase (most of them theological or philosophical, but I also noticed what seemed to be a complete set of Agatha Christies); I was studying the eight paintings disposed about the room (three were clerical portraits, the rest landscapes, clearly of this part of Ontario), when the Bishop bustled in.

"Oh, you recognize that one, of course, it's just along the lake from your place, quite a good painting, that, by a talented young local artist, Oliver Moodie, well he *was* young when he painted it, he's dead now, but some of his paintings are in the National Gallery, so good to meet you, Mr McKnight, so good of you to come to dinner at such short notice."

We shook hands; his grip was firm. "Thank you for the invitation, Your Excellency."

"Oh, none of that 'Your Excellency' stuff, that's only for business, I'm Mike to my friends, and I know you are one, may I call you Steven, do sit down again and we'll have a sherry before we go through for dinner, dry or sweet? Jeremy seems to have made a good fist of the fire, but he never remembers to put the screen in front of it, one day this whole place will burn down, and we won't even be able to blame it on Satan."

Minutes later, I had to swallow most of my sherry hastily and follow the Bishop out of the room. "We're late, my fault entirely, that damn long-distance call, why couldn't they wait for my letter, but Sister Alma will crack her whip if we don't hasten to the repast she has prepared." And indeed Sister Alma, an elderly lady of severe demeanor whose black habit did not fully conceal her emaciation, gazed sternly at us as we entered the dining-room, and as she received the Bishop's apologies, and my smile and bow when he introduced us.

Conversation was not easy, since we were separated by the candle-lit length of the oak table and interrupted frequently by Sister Alma's attentive ministrations of food and wine. Moreover, the Bishop allowed little space between his meandering speeches. But I began to glimpse how effective was his technique, for questions popped out of the flow intermittently and he listened intently to my answers – his small brown eyes fixing on me – before he seized the conversational reins again and galloped off to further rambling anecdotes, several relating to Oliver Moodie, painter of the local landscapes.

In that way, he learned – or confirmed – the following facts: that my father was indeed the celebrated newspaper magnate Munro McKnight, who had died a year ago, and who had willed his fortune to my brother William, sister Eileen, and myself; that I am thirty-three and Bill thirty-eight; that Bill is the "practical one" who is now in control of the McKnight "empire", while I, the "artistic one", have opted to continue my career as a CBC broadcaster, freelance reporter and *Globe and Mail* columnist; that I have moved from Toronto with my partner Garth into Lakeside, the big country-house that Father built in the 1950s – only about ten kilometers from Bishops Mount, as the Bishop – Mike – observed; that I feel Lakeside is my "true home" because I spent so many family holidays there as a boy – indeed most of my summers; that I was brought up Presbyterian but am now agnostic (the Bishop raised his eyebrows, but did not comment); and that Garth and I hope he will soon come to dine with us at Lakeside.

"Oh, indeed, indeed, I would enjoy that greatly, just call Sister Alma and she will identify a free evening, we must hope the weather remains mild, tonight's snowfall notwithstanding, and now we will proceed to coffee, that was a splendid dinner, Sister, the beef a trifle underdone but I know that was in honour of my new dentures, the soup and dessert delicious, as always."

I thanked her, too, as she stood aside for us at the door; she inclined her head graciously.

In the dining-room, sitting very close together on one of the couches, and talking to each other in low voices, their heads almost touching, were Fathers Piers and Jeremy. "So they're close friends, maybe even lovers?" I thought, with little surprise, and indeed with a spurt of relief.

I should mention here that I had known Piers for about five years, as an old friend of Garth's – they met at their posh Catholic college and, as Garth told it, "fell into each other's arms". Subsequently they had lost touch with each other, as Garth became a successful business-man: after leaving his university's business-school, he became one of my Father's proteges, and soon afterwards CEO of one of the flagship McKnight companies; in fact, that's how I met him. At the time, when I was in my mid-twenties, and before my rebellion against "big business", Father still hoped to inveigle me onto the Board, so, in the summer after my graduation, I had been denominated his "Private Secretary" and followed him about. During a staff Christmas party, Garth and I "fell into each other's arms", in the most literal, if rather drunken, way; and, that evening, became lovers. A week or so later, at a restaurant in the Village, Garth introduced me to Piers, who had appeared suddenly at our table, whispered in his ear, and embraced him from behind. Was I jealous? Apprehensive, rather, though Garth assured me later that Piers was "an old flame", who, after several other relationships, had "discovered his vocation to become a Catholic priest" and was now "studying for the priesthood" at a Toronto seminary. But still, Piers is very attractive, I told myself.

Garth's AIDS, when we had been together for four years, was an unexpected blow. He had been feeling increasingly ill for several months (and there were other signs that I must have concealed from myself). His Doctor sent him for the test, and, when he learned he was HIV-positive, the shock was mine more than his. I had never so much as imagined the possibility, for either of us – after all, we had both been "careful" during bathhouse visits (though Garth did later confess to "occasional bare-backing"). "You'll leave me," he said mournfully. "Of course I won't – never, Garth, never. I love you." "But you *should* leave me, my dear. Why should *you* be dragged down by it when it's all my fault?" And there were times, as the disease deepened into full-blown AIDS, when I was tempted to follow his advice; even though I saved myself from the hardest of the physical demands by hiring a first-class nurse – who quickly became as totally dedicated to serving Garth as Sister Alma is to serving the Bishop.

The move to Lakeside, and so to country-living, was in part my attempt to shelter Garth as far as possible from the pressures and distractions of the city, while giving him new interests. Besides, he had become increasingly religious, seizing on his Catholic past; and, when I broached the move, and described the house and estate, he said excitedly "But that's not far from the Cathedral where Piers is a Priest! You remember, he called last week, said he'd heard that I was sick and he was praying for me. Maybe they'll let me help as a Volunteer – and we can go to Mass on Sundays." "Well, *you* can. I'll happily drive you over. But don't expect to convert me! I'm a happy humanist."

However, by the time we were settled in, he was noticeably declining. I would often drive him over to the Cathedral, as promised, and he would spend the morning doing whatever small tasks were within his capacity, or so he told me; but I suspected, unworthily, that he spent much of the time with Piers, as he would sometimes talk glowingly, while I drove him home, about their "long philosophical conversations". But, increasingly, he was silent in the car, exhausted; and would then sleep until late in the afternoon. Piers would visit occasionally in the evenings and have supper with us. I would leave the two of them chattering together and try to get on with some work at my computer (it was probably part of Piers' plan to give me that relief from hospitality, but I actually felt a guilty jealousy!).

As the Bishop and I entered the living-room, Piers leaped up to put more logs on the fire, while Jeremy leaned forward to pour coffee into four cups. The Bishop took Piers' place beside Jeremy. "How do you like your coffee, Mr McKnight?" Jeremy asked, as I sat down on the second couch.

"Steven, Jeremy. Please call me Steven. Black, no sugar, please."

While the coffee was being dispensed, Piers sat down beside me, and we all four fell into a comfortable silence while we sipped. Then the Bishop said "Do you play card-games, Steven? If you play Bridge, I shall thank the Lord with a loud voice, but if not, we can teach you Jeremy's illicit version of 'Texas Hold 'em Up', I call it illicit because it is designed to confuse his opponents with ever-changing rules of play, which is why no betting is permitted."

"I'd love to play, Mike, thanks, but – Well, it's almost nine-thirty, and I promised Garth I'd be home before ten. There's the dogs to be fed and taken for a walk, and Garth will need to be – It's Eleanor's free night and she's spending it with her sister in Peterborough –"

Piers put an arm round my neck, pulled me to him, and kissed me. I pulled away, surprised, and he said softly "Steven, it's all been arranged. You're spending the night here, so just don't worry. And I have to tell you that the snow is quite deep now, the roads are slippery, I had to drive very carefully, and even then I nearly ended up in the ditch."

"What do you mean, 'arranged'? I can't possibly spend the night –"

"Where do you think I've been while you and Mike were having dinner? You and I actually passed each other on the road, but you didn't notice me. I was on the way to Lakeside, by arrangement with Garth. Who loves you very deeply, Steven – so deeply that he told me he felt very concerned about you; he said you had become virtually a prisoner of his AIDS, finding it hard to do your writing and broadcasting, losing your enjoyment in life, getting out of the house only rarely, mostly to drive him to and from the Cathedral, and, worst of all, getting no sex at all. So – And he said he had noticed how you and I looked at each other. Steven, he *wants* us to be together. One day last week, he said he had a plan – and that's why I drove across to your place tonight, and fed the dogs, and took them for a walk, and saw to Garth; when he'd eaten and was comfortable, I sat with him for a while, talking, and reading from *Four Quartets* to him, until he fell asleep. 'Time present and time past – ' Then I did what he'd asked me to do – switched off lights, locked the doors as I left – he promised me he would be all right until tomorrow morning and that he'd call, whatever the time, if there was any problem. Anyway, Eleanor would almost certainly be back by midnight. So –"

"So a marriage has been arranged, Steven, I offer my blessing," the Bishop said. I looked across at him, and saw I could have no doubt about his relationship with Jeremy; they were twined together, the Bishop enfolded in Jeremy's arms. "And I've put you two in the honeymoon suite," he murmured.

I drove back to Lakeside early in the morning. In spite of our intense love-making through much of the night, Piers was already up and showered when I awoke at six-thirty.

"Sorry if I disturbed you, my dear," he whispered, as he pulled on his socks. "I have a Mass at St Mark's, and it'll probably take me an hour to get there if the road's still slippery. I'd beg you to come with me if I didn't know you must get back to Garth. Give him my love, and my deepest thanks. When will I see you again?"

"Soon, please. You can always spend the night with us at Lakeside. How about tonight?"

The next three months were so intense that sometimes I felt close to collapsing. The ecstasy of my times with Piers, the suppressed sorrow of my times with Garth. Life, death, in what felt like equal but conflicting extremes. I never spent another night at Bishops Mount, but Piers would come to Lakeside two or three nights a week ("I *must* get some sleep," he would say as he left, "and that is only possible in my own bed, far removed from you"). We both spent time with Garth, too, listening to his favourite music with him, arguing about theological and political issues, petting the dogs. He was now, we had to accept, dying. What would we have done without Eleanor's devoted nursing, and the visits of the Bishop's doctor, who was exceptionally sympathetic as well as proficient? Garth's suffering, although terrible to see, was reduced as much as possible by drugs.

His birthday was the 14th of August. "I'm a Leo, I'm a Leo, so don't mess with me," he would growl loudly when I irritated him during our early days together. Now, as his birthday neared, I asked him how he would like to celebrate it (both of us secretly thinking, I'm sure, that it would be his last). "A party," he whispered huskily. "Here?" I asked. "Yes, with Piers and Jeremy and the others. All of them."

I consulted Piers. "'All of them'? He must be thinking of all the young gay priests and brothers he's met at the Cathedral. That would make a guest-list of fifteen or sixteen. Could you handle that?"

"Of course. Whatever Garth wants. Maybe I'll hire caterers. It must be the best party ever!"

"Yes, but you won't invite outsiders, will you, or any of your media friends?"

"No, of course not. No. We can have others over before or after – his parents and sister and any other relatives he wants, and my brother and sister, and my mother, who adores him. His Toronto friends. Sounds like a second party! I'll work it out with Garth. What about the Bishop – Mike – do you think he'd like to come to our party?"

"I doubt if he'll have the time. He seems to be very thick with the Vatican lately, lots of calls to and fro – the new Pope seems to consult him on various issues."

"But the new Pope is extremely conservative, from all I've read and heard. The Vatican recently came out with new 'guidelines' to prevent gays being accepted in seminaries – you must know about that? 'No gay priests!' What a bad joke, when there are so many gay priests already – they are probably keeping your Church going. But Rome obviously still defines homosexual activity, if not homosexuals themselves, as 'intrinsically disordered', I think that's the phrase. How can Mike accept that? What do *you* think about that?"

"But he has to be diplomatic, Steven. He has to be careful. There's too much at stake if he rebels openly against Rome. Remember, too, the pedophile abuse scandals, Mount Cashel especially. We're still dealing with the aftermath, including the displeasure of the Vatican. And advances *are* being made, slowly, Steven. We have to be patient."

The weather was glorious for Garth's Party. When they came eagerly out of the Cathedral bus, thirteen young gay men informally dressed and ready to enjoy themselves, Garth, who was in his wheelchair, protected from the sun by a big floppy hat, smiled for the first time in days. The Doctor and Eleanor had readied him for the occasion, then discreetly departed together in his car.

"Just don't let him get too excited and tired," Eleanor had whispered to me. "Exhaustion could be dangerous, as you know."

At my suggestion, the visitors had brought swim-trunks and towels. After they had greeted Garth, one by one, kissing his forehead and touching his arms or hands, they trooped up to the house to change. Garth and I could hear their lively badinage, and smiled gently at each other. Then they came chasing each other down the patio steps and ran past us, to the glittering lake. A troop of pale but beautiful young men. Soon they were splashing about boisterously, with shrieks and bellows, and some of them swam out to the floating deck to wrestle and sunbathe. Several (and ultimately all of them) shed their trunks and capered about on the beach naked, while our two spaniels, Charles and Diana, gamboled and yapped around them.

"Like a herd of adolescent schoolboys," I heard behind me, and the Bishop sat down heavily in a garden-chair beside Garth. "Happy Birthday, Garth, is it too soon to give you my present, no doubt it is, but I can stay only a short while, I have a problem in the Cathedral I must deal with, so would you mind?" I unwrapped the gift and held it up for Garth to see. It was a framed print of a painting by Oliver Moodie. "Look, it's this very view, across the lake, I thought you would like to have it, can you see Bishops Mount, on the right, of course the trees were much smaller, you can't see much of the building now from here, as you have noticed, and in his time there were no high-rises in the distance. He must have been painting at his easel, standing here, just about where we are sitting right now."

"Lovely," Garth whispered. "Thank you, Mike."

Piers and Jeremy now appeared with fruit juice for us, and then set about preparing the picnic tables for the open-air meal I had decided upon, with their advice and the co-operatively warm, dry weather.

"Perhaps this would be a good moment, if you don't mind, Garth, for me to be guided by Steven through his splendid house?"

As I showed him round, the Bishop asked many questions and commented admiringly on all he saw. "Do you know, Steven, I'm sorry I didn't manage to visit you before now, I have so often looked across the lake to this building, and thought, with I must confess some jealousy, that it looked as if it would make an ideal monastery, and now that I have seen it, inside as well as out, and seen the delight, too, of my young priests as they enjoy its surroundings, I know that I was right, I know that my vision came to me from the Saints, perhaps from the Virgin Mary, who watches over our Cathedral and all who serve God in this diocese."

He stopped and turned. His small brown eyes focused sharply

on me, and he reached out both hands to take mine. "Steven," he said solemnly, "I want to express my deep gratitude to you, indeed the gratitude of all of us at the Cathedral, for bringing Garth among us, he is a truly exceptional man, his efforts among us, especially with the young people, and his warmth and integrity and courage, have been a blessing, and have taught us much about the strength and depth of God's love, I know that you have supported him throughout, to the utmost, Steven, and we are truly grateful. Truly he is a Saint in our midst."

When he dropped my hands, I said "Thank you, Mike. I'm so glad I've been able to help a little; Garth badly wanted to be involved with the Cathedral, and I'm so glad that has worked out so positively, for him and for you."

Our birthday meal was boisterous, the visitors becoming more and more rowdy and their jokes and anecdotes increasingly erotic. I could see that their laughter was both delighting and tiring Garth, so I called for the sparkling-cider, and, once Piers and Jeremy had filled the glasses, started my short speech (thank goodness I stopped myself, just in time, from "drinking his health" – though I fear that my momentary hesitation actually drew attention to the omission). "Let us drink to Garth, in love and gratitude – to Garth, dear friend and lover" – at which point I knew I would weep if I continued, so I lifted my glass and drank, and the others quickly followed my lead.

"And now dig into the food, guys," Piers called out. I sat down again beside Garth, with a bowl of soup which I slowly spooned into his slack mouth.

"How do you feel, my dear? Say if you want to go indoors, out of this bright light. Are you tired?"

He smiled faintly and nodded Yes. So I shouted above the din, "Garth and I are going inside. Thank you all for coming, and making Garth's birthday such a festival. Come and see us later, in Garth's bedroom, please, before you leave."

Then I lifted Garth out of the wheel-chair; he was so light now that it was easy to carry him up the steps and through to our bedroom. Outside, they were soon playing an extemporary game of baseball, with yells and expostulations. While I watched him, Garth sighed deeply, and fell asleep. Holding his hand, I dozed.

In the late afternoon, they came to say goodbye, all thirteen of the young gay priests or brothers; in couples or singly. Garth still slept, so I thanked them briefly on his behalf as they came quietly to kiss his damp forehead. After them came Piers and Jeremy. "We'll just see all the guys onto the bus," Piers said, "then we'll tidy up and wash up."

"He's fast asleep," I replied, "so I can come and help you. I hope you know how truly grateful I am to you both for all you have done to make this such a glorious occasion."

Garth died that night, so there was no second party – it had been arranged for a few days later, to give him time to recover from the first. When she returned, Eleanor had been worried about Garth's state; the Doctor, Nigel, came in with her, and injected morphine shortly before Garth suffered several spasms, and died in my arms.

Perhaps it was as well, for me, that I had to spend so much time and energy telephoning and e-mailing next day – his family, my family, our friends, the Cathedral. To Eleanor I said "I feel so guilty, it must all have been too much for him yesterday", but she responded, "No, he didn't have much longer anyway, and the Birthday Party was a wonderful farewell. I think he died happy, Steven, or as happy as possible – that's what you and the Boys gave him." I hope she was right. I also started digging his grave that day, sweating and weeping.

The funeral was a simple burial ceremony at Lakeside, a few days after Garth's death. It was conducted by Piers and Jeremy, beside his grave in front of the house, where Garth had requested he be buried, "so I can look out at the lake forever". (Support from the Bishop made the necessary local-authority permission a formality.) Besides Piers, Garth, and myself, only Eleanor and Nigel, the Doctor, were present. We wept together, and afterwards had a scratch supper together.

The Bishop arranged a Memorial Mass at the Cathedral for the following Saturday. Friends and family members drove here from Toronto, and were joined, for the ceremony and reception, by many members of the Cathedral's congregation. So it was a splendid occasion, replete with the grandiosity of spectacular robes, processions, thundering organ, the smell of incense, and a soaring funeral oration by the Bishop, who presided over the service, with Piers and Jeremy as his assistants ("Quite a send-off for a little gay boy!" I imagined Garth whispering to me). I drifted through it all as if stunned into meditative silence.

Two weeks later, I was sitting on the garden-seat near Garth's grave (which still lacked the marble headstone I had ordered). It was a superb Fall afternoon, yellow and brown leaves spinning around me, the sun sinking into a bed of soft pink cloud above the lake.

"Hullo, Steve." It was Jeremy. He sat down beside me. "How're you doing?"

"Oh, getting back into my regular life, I guess. Slowly."

"Well, it's hard. If I can do anything to help, please – Why don't you come over to the Cathedral and I can introduce you to some of the guys Garth worked with?"

"I'm all right, Jeremy. I know it takes time. I still see and hear him, you know. I was just remembering how he whispered to me, on the day of his Birthday Party – we were sitting out here and the Boys were having a good time swimming and running about – He winked at me and whispered, I could hardly hear him, 'Look thy last on all things lovely."

"And who – ? That's a quotation, isn't it?"

"Yes, I looked it up in our *Oxford Book of Quotations*. It's from a poem by Walter de la Mare, an English poet. It's beautiful, isn't it? 'Look thy last on all things lovely'. My favourite poet, and Garth's, was T.S. Eliot – he loved *Four Quartets* almost too deeply. Do you have a favourite poet?"

"The alliteration, all those liquid 'L's, that's what makes the line so memorable. Yes – I guess it should be Hopkins, but I don't care for him – it's Walt Whitman, though I haven't read him for years. 'I mourned, and yet shall mourn with ever-returning spring' – somehow I remember that line, though don't ask me which poem it comes from."

"Garth's quotation comes from a poem called 'Fare Well'. I've been wondering if he was trying to tell me he knew he was close to death and was saying goodbye. 'Fare Well.' And I was too obtuse to get it. But maybe not, maybe Garth didn't know or remember the poem's title."

"Or maybe he was just ready to go, that day, and told God, and God was merciful and said 'Come'. So many unanswered questions after any death. For the survivors."

"So, move on? That's what I'm trying to do. I'm back to my daily writing routine, anyway. How is Piers? I thought he'd call or come over, but no, silence. I've assumed that he and you and the Bishop – Mike – were giving me space to mourn – but it seems a long time since I saw him."

"Well – Actually, Piers isn't here any more. Mike sent him to work in a parish in Windsor a few days ago. Said he needed new challenges."

"Windsor? But he didn't tell me, he didn't even say goodbye."

"Because Mike forbade him to contact you. Mike made him take a vow of silence."

"And Piers accepted that?"

"Steve, can we go inside? It's getting cold, and soon it'll be dark. I have to talk to you."

As we sat drinking coffee, Jeremy finally broke a long silence. "You see, Steve, Mike is deeply hurt and offended, and he blamed Piers, even more than you, for what's happened."

"And what is that, Jeremy? I don't understand any of this."

"Your article. It was your column in last Saturday's *Globe and Mail*."

"But that was all positive – as positive as I could make it, the most complimentary I have ever been, one of my colleagues said. About the Cathedral and all it had meant to Garth, about Mike as the best Bishop ever, about the Boys and their goodness and vitality –"

"That was the problem, Steve. It's what I told Mike – I told him that you didn't do it deliberately, you wouldn't ever have imagined the consequences. He said Piers should have made it very clear to you that everything here was private and not for public knowledge. Piers says he did warn you. What a mess! Also, and this is confidential too, there was a good chance that the Pope would name the Archbishop of Toronto a Cardinal, he and Mike are very close – Mike has had excellent relations with the new Pope and the Vatican, as I think you know. Now, Mike says – Well, the other day I saw a report that the Pope had named about twenty new cardinals, and when I saw that the Archbishop wasn't one of them, I didn't dare say anything to Mike. I know this is all Church politics, Steve, and hypocrisy, yes – but surely you can see why Mike is so upset? He thinks that you have spilled the beans about how it is here, and the publicity is sure to cause problems, especially if it reaches Rome. He says he may himself be forced to move now, to somewhere more remote. Then what will happen here, under a new Bishop?"

"And all because I wrote a column in praise of the open, generous acceptance of gay priests and brothers in this diocese. And because I wrote that I wish this could happen elsewhere, and argued that it pointed to the best and strongest and most *Christian* solution to the problems your Church has been facing – pedophile priests, Mount Cashel, sexual abuse of choirboys, and so on and so on. Good God, Jeremy! We are only human, you, me, Piers, Mike, all of us – we are human males, sexual animals, and we need to express and fulfill ourselves sexually if we are going to be able to strive for the spiritual. We can't live isolated from each other. Of course a great many priests and brothers are gay – why try to pretend otherwise, why punish those very men who are drawn to the priesthood, who give themselves, their sensitivity and tenderness, their very need to love others, to God and the Church? Who are probably the *backbone* of your Church. And, anyway, I bet noone has complained locally. I didn't use any names or local references – surely Mike saw that?"

I found myself weeping – whether in humiliation or anger, or because of Garth and Piers and myself. And Jeremy. He came to me, hugged me, and kissed me.

"Steve, I have something else to tell you. I've resigned as Mike's Chaplain – if 'resigned' is the right word – I wrote him a note just before I came over here, saying I couldn't continue. I think he'll be glad to be rid of me. He never respected my spiritual advice anyway."

"But – then what happens? What will you do?"

"Move in with you. If you'll have me." He smiled.

I looked into his steady green eyes. "Of course. Of course, Jeremy. Stay as long as you like."

"There's more to it, as I'm sure you'd guess. Mike has a new lover, Brother Greg. Mike found him somewhere, or he found Mike, a month or so ago, and Mike brought him to help in the garden at Bishops Mount. In addition to being very beautiful, he's a nice young boy – actually, he came to Garth's Birthday Party, and it was only then, when I noticed how he reacted to Mike's unexpected arrival, that the penny dropped. But I always knew it was only a matter of time. When I arrived here, I heard, from some of my fellow-priests, that Mike always wanted beautiful young men, and when each one got older he was replaced by a younger one – just as with me. There's also the story about Oliver Moodie, the painter. Apparently he and Mike were lovers when they were young, then Mike left him when he was called to the priesthood. Oliver never recovered. He threw himself into painting, and was making a name for himself; but then he appeared here soon after Mike arrived as Bishop, more than twenty years ago. Mike would have nothing to do with him, and finally he committed suicide – drowned himself in the lake. So I knew very well how – callous Mike can be."

"Oh – I'm sorry, Jeremy. That's a very sad story. Thank you for being so honest about yourself. I guess you and I are both widows.

In fact, I'm a double widow, now that Piers has gone. So we should comfort each other – who knows, we may fall in love. I think I'm halfway there – we've shared a lot in a short time, haven't we? – and I've always liked and admired you, Jeremy. But I'm thinking of moving back to Toronto – would you come and live with me there?"

"And I liked you from the moment we met last winter, Steve. Yes, I would. But what will you do with Lakeside?"

"Well – Mike made it very clear that it would make a fine monastery. I could donate it to the diocese?"

"Oh, that reminds me. I'd forgotten that I have another message from Mike, and a letter to give you on behalf of the Cathedral. To thank you very much for your extremely generous gift of $500,000, in memory of Garth. They would like to know, but this isn't urgent, if you want to stipulate that any of the money be spent on a particular project."

"No. I'll reply that they should use the money as they decide – which I think is what Garth would want. He didn't believe in conditions and restrictions. How about some supper? If I'm hungry, you must be ravenous – being so much younger than me. Ten years?"

Boiled eggs and toast, followed by marmalade and toast; on our laps in front of the fire.

"As you've just seen, Jeremy, I'm not a great cook, I can only do basics. Eleanor's been doing most of the cooking. Shall we get back to *our* basics, the basics of our future lives? Lakeside – do I give it to the diocese?"

"No, you don't. Mike was right: it *would* make a fine monastery. But why don't we turn it into a new type of monastery? – a home and refuge for gay priests and brothers of this diocese, and maybe for retired gay priests, and – nuns too – maybe also a retreat centre – I'm just thinking this out as I talk, Steve, on the lines you were suggesting. That could really make a big difference in the diocese, don't you think? And even in the Church generally – change has got to come."

"What support do you think we'd get? How about the nuns, for instance?"

"Oh, they will certainly be there for us. Some of them are lesbians, I'm sure, and those who aren't have often fled male domination and violence – they don't like heterosexual male arrogance, and they obviously enjoy the company of young gay priests, and working with them – the maternal impulse, I guess, to some extent. Once, when I was helping Sister Alma in the kitchen, she suddenly pointed at my crotch and said 'You boys got a lotta mischief down there' and I said 'What do you mean?' and she said 'You know what I mean, you boys have lotta fun together, good.' I just hope *they* have some fun together. They seem to judge us indulgently, many of them, as if we're the sons they never had – and they generally seem to consider men to be naughty by nature, needing their silly little erections and sexual spasms. Of course I'm generalizing madly. But I do think they would support what we're proposing, as long as we don't rock the boat too much."

"What *you're* proposing, my dear Jeremy. I'm beginning to see that you are hoping to exploit me and my millions just as much as dear Mike ever did. And I'm not even a Catholic! Don't forget that."

"Oh, I don't, not for a moment. You are my next convert, Steve. It is ordained. Mike said so. And you know Garth would approve. Then all will be joy, and your many Presbyterian sins will be forgiven. – Oh, talking of joy, has Eleanor spoken to you recently?"

"Yes – just yesterday, in fact. About another proposal – this one by Nigel to Eleanor."

"She called and asked if I would marry them. Of course, she made it clear that I was her second choice, after Piers. 'He knew Garth much longer than you,' she said, 'but you gave Garth love and support too – and anyway, Piers isn't here – but maybe he will come and you can do it together.' So I said Yes, as long as the wedding is at Lakeside. 'Oh, yes, it must be there, outside in the garden, close to Garth's grave, next summer – I know Steven will agree.' I added that I hope they will always live near us, and she said she hoped so too.

Nigel would be a great doctor for our Monastery, and, as you know, Eleanor is a great cook as well as a superb nurse."

"'Near *us*', Jeremy? – When you said that to her, you hadn't even proposed to me yet! Wretch! Come here."

All shall be well and all shall be well and all manner of thing shall be well.

Bravo, Ms Austen!

"Cousin Frederick! What a surprise! I could not believe it when you were announced. Cassandra and I were about our toilettes, and the house is at sixes and sevens on account of –"

"Forgive me, Jane, for visiting at this early hour. It is because Mamma –"

"Not another word! I will not hear another word!"

"But I must, Cousin, I must. Mamma has –"

"I know what you are about to say, Cousin. I will not listen, I will not listen. See, I cover both ears with my hands! It will be un-acceptable, an unforgivable breach of decorum and family unity, as well as a deadly insult to both brother Edward and me. Your presence at the Ball tonight is essential. As you well know, Edward is providing it, at great expense, in honour of our entry into his neighbourly circle, as well as the publication of my *Pride and Prejudice*, and you will, as always, be expected to be the life and soul of the occasion –"

"Not tonight, dear Cousin. I would be in misery. I would refuse to converse with anyone, I would cut all your favourite friends, even Mrs. Lefroy –"

"Now you jest, Frederick. You know you are not capable of such unsociable behaviour. That would be too, too like my dear Darcy –"

"Yes, and that is behind Mamma's summons, Jane, I know it. Not that I am in any way Mr. Darcy, but –"

"No, you have not yet appeared in my writings, Frederick, so be warned! Anything you say and do now will be remembered and used against you –"

"Jane, please listen to me. Mamma has been reading *Pride and Prejudice* and she is in a fury, convinced that she has been traduced in your characterisation of Lady Catherine de Bourgh. She tells me in the letter I received last night that she intends to confront you with the evidence. She also believes that your obnoxiously obsequi-ous Mr. Collins is based on Father. If that is so, *I* shall be offended too. You know how generous and kind Father always was, to you and all his relatives."

"Well, she may confront me if she wishes – just as Lady de Bourgh confronted my Lizzy. I would of course deny that Lady de Bourgh, like Mr. Collins, is a portrait of any person. All my characters are airy creatures of the imagination, though of course with roots in reality. What will you tell her, Cousin?"

"I will tell Mamma quite that, Jane, though not so prettily or mendaciously. I am not an Author. I will warn her, too, that if she confronts you she will surely rue it, and later recognise herself as one of your most ridiculous future characters."

"Bravo! Shall we sit, Cousin? I see that my breakfast will have to wait as I continue to enforce your submission. Have you eaten? Oh yes, of course you have: no Man would brave his favourite Cousin's wrath on an empty stomach!"

"Jane, you may laugh at me in your unsympathetic way; nevertheless, my situation is distressing. Mamma is threatening to disown me, and cut me completely out of her Will, if I do not return immediately to London."

"As she has done before, Frederick. It is her way. Courage! You are her only son, you are the apple of her eye: she would never carry through with her threat. That is your advantage, an undeserved one I admit, but –"

"I cannot take the risk, Jane. Three thousand pounds a year! How would I live?"

"With difficulty and in penury, like some of the rest of us, my dear Frederick. And it would do you good! Yet as you are a Man, rather than a mere female, like some of us, the world would be your oyster. Think of it: you could actually earn your living!"

"You know my wish is to be ordained as a Clergyman, Cousin – but for that I need Mamma's money and the patronage she commands. But I see you are succeeding in distracting me from my purpose in visiting you this morning."

"Now let me tell you my Plan, Cousin Frederick. Of course, you know I have one."

"But how could you – ?"

"Because I know your Mamma, my very esteemed Aunt, almost as well as I know Lady Catherine de Bourgh. I know too that she does not like to imagine you enjoying yourself and putting yourself in romantic danger near me."

"'Romantic danger – near you'? Surely you do not think – ?"

"Indeed I do not, Cousin! I do not! I noticed the way you looked at – I will refrain from saying 'stared at' – Mrs. Lefroy's handsome Irish nephew when we were playing cards and dancing at her house the other night. I noticed the exchange of significant glances between you and Mr. Lefroy. Yes, you may well blush! I know your secret, Cousin! You can conceal nothing from me."

"That is cruel, Cousin!"

"No, Frederick, it is merely honest – and sharply-observed in the way for which I shall become famous. Papa assured me so, when I was a mere slip of a girl. But again I distract you, and myself. Let me elucidate my Plan for your applause. My card is already filled for tonight, top and bottom. You are top and Mr. Lefroy is bottom – and I hope for dances with both of you, in the middle, if you are not exhausted by then."

"But, Jane, everyone knows you are in love with Mr. Lefroy and he with you."

"So you will appreciate my cunning, Cousin. Indeed, I do *not* love Mr. Lefroy, believe me; but he is a superlative dance-partner. That is what I love! In himself, Mr. Lefroy is so excessively ambitious, humourlessly egocentric, and, worst of all, loquacious – I barely get in one *bon mot* each dance while he whirls me about in his Irish way, talking continuously, and unnecessarily loudly, into whichever ear happens to be passing by his mouth. And consider what a horror it would be, to be condemned to live in Ireland! And to be condemned to produce an annual child! And to be so far from the loving admiration of my family – including you, my dearest Cousin! No, it cannot be. And I will tell Mr Lefroy so when I next identify a pause in his speech – for even he must draw breath occasionally."

"Please, dear Jane. Be serious."

"Since dear Papa's death, I am notoriously serious, Cousin. Everyone notices it. In Bath, during his illness and after his death, it was impossible for me to write. But now I can again; I can, I can. The joy of living here at Chawton! And though inexpressibly serious, I am still dizzy with delight; so forgive my levity, Cousin – displayed only to you, as I trust you excessively. Indeed, as a tribute to you, and the complexity of your personality, I am splitting you into two in the very serious novel I am in the course of writing: you will be both of its heroes, Frederick – but only if you agree to neglect your imperious Mamma for one more night."

"Jane, Jane! You are *not* being serious!"

"I am never more serious than when I am being humorous, dear Frederick. It is called Irony. I will be famous for that too."

"Jane, Jane. There is no time for Irony. I must communicate imminently with Mamma –"

"And besides, I am very content living here as a Woman with my dear Cassandra. I assure you that my daily life with her has its humble pleasures, just as you, I must assume, find lively enjoyment with members of your own less-domesticated sex. It is a situation that permits me to be the Author I am determined to be, and will always be determined to be. Here, when not dancing, I can sit meekly in my corner – quiet, mousy Jane listening and observing, quite undetected – and then I can turn much of that nonsense into novels; after I have first read everything I write to my dearest but very critical Sister, and revised it closely in the light of her opinion. Do you not agree that this is an ideal life and creative process for an impoverished but respectable gentlewoman who wishes merely to entertain, and to be famous after her death – and make some pocket-money before that?"

"I am beginning to feel that I am being whirled about in an Irish way while Mr. Lefroy converses endlessly with my ear! Is no rescue possible?"

"Ah, yes: Mr. Lefroy. And you, dear Frederick, my precious but abused and frustrated Cousin. We must get you two together, where you will give and receive the great enjoyment I know you both anxiously desire. And so, my Plan. I have arranged with Cassandra, who thoroughly approves of it, that our dressing-room upstairs in Godmersham will be available for you and Mr. Lefroy to utilise during the Ball tonight. After you have spectactularly opened the dancing as my partner, and Mr. Lefroy has very prominently danced with the unbearably wealthy Miss Edith Mooney, you will both repair unnoticed to the dressing-room, and there enjoy each other's company in whichever way you please, until I knock softly at the door to warn you that your renewed presence is required downstairs. Mr. Lefroy's absence, I am sorry to say, will probably be noticed long before yours, Cousin! What do you think? Is it not a practicable Plan, as well as delightful in what it provides for your enjoyment?"

"Jane, soon it will be too late for me to send an answer to Mamma. And your breakfast will be cold."

"Indeed, I care not for the state of my boiled eggs, but am filled with joy to know you have agreed to be present at the Ball."

"Now, Jane –"

"No more chatter, Cousin. All is arranged satisfactorily. My advice is that you thoroughly enjoy yourself with Mr. Lefroy tonight, then, before the Ball ends, propose to the unbearably wealthy Miss Edith Mooney; and after your marriage to her, father at least three lively, witty young ladies for me to train up as Authors. The future of the Novel is Feminine: I and Fanny Burney, Maria Edgworth, and a few other literary females have so ordained. Even Sir Walter Scott admits that. All we need is a contingent of aspiring female Authors to admire us, and learn from us, and follow our example; and that is where you and a few other intelligent and imaginative Men may play a significant supporting role, like that played by my dearly beloved Father."

"Jane –"

"I believe it is time for my breakfast, Cousin; and time for you to gallop back to Godmersham. Pray give our greetings to Edward and

Elizabeth. I am delighted that you decided to visit our humble abode so early on this notable day, and that you will be in attendance at the Ball tonight."

With apologies to all Janeites, who will long before now have recognised the outrageous liberties I have taken with Austen's biography. Characters and events have been tossed about, and even invented, in what I hope she would approve as creative fiction loosely based on selected scraps of actuality. I like to think that she would enjoy reading the Dialogue above as much as its Author has enjoyed writing it. Bravo, great Jane!

The Hudson Affair

It is another foggy London day. As they pass along Baker Street, the shadowy horses drawing shadowy hansoms transporting shadowy members of the aristocracy to aristocratic destinations cast into the damp dirty air a succession of hollow clip-cloppings. In the swirling murk there lurk multiple malefactors and their soon-to-be victims – murderers and future corpses; rapists and lovely, unwise virgins; pickpockets and wealthy, unobservant, elderly gentlemen; lawyers and politicians.

Hurrying to the front door of my friend Sherlock Holmes' lodgings, I try not to look over my shoulder – and flinch away, probably just in time, from a rushing vehicle. Reaching the door safely, I ring its bell – several times – before drawing forth a large key and inserting it in the keyhole. Where is Mrs Hudson, Holmes' housekeeper and cook?

Once inside, I call out "Holmes, I am here", before becoming aware of the thin tones of his violin. I climb heavily up the stairs to Holmes' study, whence emanate the sounds. After knocking gently without result, I push the door open and enter.

There is Holmes, seated just beyond his always-untidy desk, his raised eyes closed, his right arm pulsating rhythmically as a plaintive melody lifts from the strings. Long experience has taught me that only silence is an acceptable response, so I stand, waiting to be noticed. The music sinks slowly to a closing cadence. Then, at last, Holmes opens his eyes and the violin is placed carefully in its case.

Holmes speaks, languorously. "'If music be the food of love, play on, give me excess of it.' What do I mean, Watson?'

"Are you in love, Holmes?"

"No, no," says he, sighing, "that is not what I meant. Alas, Watson, no suitable amorous admirer has appeared yet this morning – say, a very beautiful Russian Princess weeping lasciviously because her priceless tiara and necklace are mysteriously absent. But the day is young. Who knows what excitements await me? Unless I starve first."

"'Starve', Holmes? Have you not taken breakfast?"

"Watson, *that* was my meaning. An excess of metaphorical food implies the absence of actual food. Is that not obvious? I have not eaten for at least a day. Indeed, only cocaine has quelled the quiverings of mind and body. Would you be so kind as to descend to the kitchen, and prepare tea and sandwiches for me? Then we shall talk."

"I came as soon as I received your telegram," say I. "It is extremely foggy this morning, so it was advisable to take extraordinary care. But where is Mrs Hudson? When she did not answer the door-bell, I assumed she was busy in the kitchen, or elsewhere in the house."

"For the second day, Mrs Hudson has not arrived. We shall talk of this over breakfast, my dear Watson. Have mercy on my innards."

After bumping around in Mrs Hudson's domain – which, I smile to myself, Holmes has probably never penetrated – I am able to send upwards, via the dumb-waiter, an abbreviated repast consisting of boiled eggs, toast and of course tea. When I puff back into the study, I find Holmes attacking the eggs and toast with fervour. We eat in silence. Naturally, Holmes is too preoccupied to express – perhaps even to feel – gratitude.

When we have finished eating, I hazard "About Mrs Hudson, Holmes? Is she ill? I devoutly hope not."

"Not ill, apparently, so much as angry and hurt."

"Oh, Holmes, surely you did not – ?"

"Watson, I am surprised at you. I have always treated Mrs Hudson with the greatest respect, delicacy and appreciation. Others, it seems from what she wrote in the note delivered yesterday morning, have not. I also pay her well for her labours in this place."

"Well, then – ?" say I.

"Well, then." He reaches for what is obviously Mrs Hudson's note. "She writes here that she is deeply disturbed, with physical consequences of prostration, by a discovery she made, quite by chance. Two days ago, while she was gathering her husband's clothing for the wash, she noticed, as it fell out of a pocket, the incomplete draft of what was to become a letter to – whom?"

"'Whom'? Was there no salutation?"

"Yes, but not including a name. Merely 'My dearest – Blank.'"

"What was the purport of the letter? A debt unpaid – he requesting more time? A Letter to the Editor of the *Pall Mall Gazette* or *The Times*?"

"No, no, Watson. Unless Mrs Hudson, whose literary capacity is of course limited, has misread or misinterpreted the document, it expresses a meaning very different – and quite unexpected, she said. In fact, by her account and reaction, it is a love-letter. I hesitate to say more about it, since I have not seen the letter. The Hudsons have been married thirty-two years – she mentions that in her note – and produced two children, one of whom, her daughter Agatha, is living with them after her husband was killed in a street accident. As you say, Watson, it is necessary to take great care, as a pedestrian, on our streets now. Especially in the fog."

"But, Holmes, what exactly does Mrs Hudson say about the letter's contents? Why was she so disturbed by what she read?"

"That is what you will find out, Watson."

"I, Holmes? It is unlikely that she would wish to speak to me about what would seem to be a very private matter. Why do not you question her? Her note was addressed to you alone. If she cannot or will not come here, could not you invite her to meet you in a coffee-house – ?"

"I am too weak to leave this house, Watson, after such extreme food deprivation. Surely you have noted my emaciation and poor enunciation? No, *you* must go. Immediately. This is a serious situation which must be satisfactorily resolved as soon as possible, my dear friend. Surely you can appreciate that?"

"Well –" say I.

"I know you will treat the matter with your usual tact and sensitivity. Ask to see the letter-draft and, after analysing it, question her as closely as you can. If you think it appropriate, arrange to speak to her husband too. As you know, he works as a bank-clerk in the City. I do not need to say that discovering the name of the letter's proposed recipient is likely to be the key that unlocks this mystery, and will send Mrs Hudson back where she is so greatly appreciated, and so greatly missed. As I say, please be extremely tactful, and employ all your considerable charm."

After several hours of travel by hansom, and after local enquiries, I locate the residence of Mr and Mrs Walter Hudson, in an Islington street. Mrs Hudson is startled by my appearing at her front door, but of course invites me in for tea.

As we are sitting comfortably in her parlour, with a fire warming us, I gently raise the matter of her absence from Baker Street, stressing Holmes' sadness, and inability to function domestically without her valued assistance.

Mrs Hudson bursts into tears. "Oh, Sir," she gasps, after recovering her equanimity, and blowing her nose. "I am so very sorry to have offended the best employer any woman could desire. I beg that you offer him apologies on my behalf, and sue for his kind forgiveness and understanding. Please assure him that I will return to my employment tomorrow morning."

"Do you feel sufficiently recovered, Mrs Hudson?" I ask. "Have you been ill? If so, I would of course be happy to offer medical advice, or treatment, as appropriate."

"Oh, no, no, Sir. As I wrote in my note to Mr Holmes, the cause of my absence was the chance discovery of a letter Mr Hudson was writing. I have it here, Sir." She draws a much-folded sheet of paper from a pocket in her voluminous skirt, and hands it to me. "I have always trusted Mr Hudson so completely, Sir, that it was a dreadful shock –"

She bursts into tears again, and sniffles into a handkerchief while I peruse what indeed seems to be the beginning of a love-letter. 'I have so greatly missed you, my dearest one. I long to be with you again, as soon as possible. Why did you not come last week? I cannot endure another such disappointment. Will we meet this week? Is there no possibility of another, safer meeting-place?' At which point, the draft-letter ends.

"Mrs Hudson", say I gently. "Do you know for whom this missive was intended?"

"No, Sir. Mr Hudson always said he would never even look at another woman, let alone – I have maddened myself thinking about unattached women along this street, or women he may have encountered in our local pub –"

"Have you not spoken about this matter to Mr Hudson?"

"Not yet, Sir. I intend to speak to him tonight, when he is settled in front of the fire after dinner. To be honest, Sir, I have been very uncertain about how to act for the best. I must consider my daughter Agatha, who is living with us, and my son in Southampton and his family – our three grandchildren –" She looked pleadingly at me. "If you do not mind my asking, Sir, what would you advise?"

"Do you wish to leave Mr Hudson?"

"Oh, no, Sir. He has been a good husband, and I never had call to complain before now."

"Well, then, Mrs Hudson", say I, after a pause for reflection. "It occurs to me that it may be for the best, in the circumstances, that you say nothing to him about the matter. A man may be misled briefly by a pretty, importunate face, but if he has a happy marriage to a wife as loving and dutiful as you, as well as beloved children and grandchildren, he will quickly come to his senses, and ensure that he is not again tempted to wander, emotionally, from home and hearth."

"Oh, Sir, I am so glad to hear you say that. I hoped you would counsel caution. I love my husband, and I believe, in spite of his moment of weakness, that he loves me too. I must also consider my widowed daughter, who is in great need of our love and support, and has just found employment as a sempstress." With that, she tears the letter into several pieces, rises, and casts the scraps into the fire; then turns to me. "I feel so relieved, Sir. Thank you for your advice. You have always been so good to me."

"Excellent advice, indeed," says Holmes, when I have finished reporting the substance of my visit to Mrs Hudson. "The incriminating letter is destroyed, its author ignorant of the danger, even disaster, that he had invited, and his wife is happy to return to the role of dutiful wife. So, all is well, and all manner of thing shall be well, Watson. *You*, especially, have done well, as I expected – I knew you were just the man for the task, my dear friend. And *I* regain my esteemed cook and housekeeper. All that appears to be missing is my dinner tonight."

"Oh, Holmes, I was about to say that I shall be dining at home tonight, and that you are most welcome to join my wife and myself for dinner."

"But how will your wife feel about that – welcoming me to a meal, when she may well suspect something odd about your activities here? She has always struck me as a most perceptive person."

"What do you mean, Holmes? My 'activities' here? How could she possibly object to my visiting my closest friend, and assisting as far as possible in solving dastardly crimes?"

Holmes fixes me with his fiercest gaze. "Do you think you can deceive me, Watson? Am I nothing but a credulous fool?"

"Again I ask, Holmes, what you can possibly mean. I am in the dark."

"Then I shall enlighten you, Watson. I noticed some time ago that you regularly visit my rooms on Friday afternoons, and proceed down to the kitchen, where you have tea with Mrs Hudson and enjoy a conversation with her and her husband, who enters through the back door at about the same time – as he does every day, ready to accompany his wife home after she has cooked and prepared the dinner. It is, as you have pronounced, and others recognise, essential to take great care when walking on London streets – any diligent husband would wish to accompany and protect his wife, especially at night, would he not?"

"True, Holmes, I enjoy the company and conversation of Mrs Hudson and her husband, when the opportunity occurs. What is amiss in that? You know that I am a gregarious person, and, like you, do not conform to the dictates of the class system. And there is time between my arrival and joining you at dinner for –"

"For what, Watson?" he interrupts me. "You told me that, while I was occupied privately in my study before dinner, playing my violin –"

"And enjoying the delights of opium?"

He ignores my interruption, and continues,"You told me that, after Mrs Hudson commenced cooking and other preparations for dinner, on Fridays, you would proceed to the parlour and read *The Times* until summoned by the bell to the table. Yet, when I have read my copy of that Friday newspaper, after your departure, I have in past weeks found it pristine, unlike earlier occasions when I was forced to reassemble it. You may not have noted that I have also, recently, tried to converse with you about major happenings reported in Friday's headlines, only to experience unwonted silence or evasion. Having established that you were not spending the hour before dinner quietly reading in the parlour, I wondered where you *were* spending it. So I scattered flour unobtrusively on the floor of the larder – flour some of which appeared later on the floor of the dining-room, obviously deposited there by your shoes."

"But Mrs Hudson goes into the larder regularly –"

"And places her shoes under the dining-room table during dinner, Watson? Moreover, as you are well aware, she would not enter the larder while cooking dinner, would she? You are silent, Watson."

I smile, with some effort. "Where is all this laborious detection taking us, Holmes?"

"To the truth, of course, Watson. One final piece of deduction first. Last Friday you were here, as usual, but the preceding Friday, I remember, you hurried in late, when I had already started eating, and said you had been called out unexpectedly to visit one of your sick aristocratic patients. That was my final clue, Watson – when it was corroborated in your account of your lover's letter."

"'Lover'? What are you talking about, Holmes" I bluster.

"Walter Hudson is your lover. His wife assumed, without question, that he was addressing the draft-letter to a *woman*. It did not occur to her, innocent as she is, that a man may fall in love with another man. But *we* know that it happens, Watson. Moreover, you deceived Mrs Hudson, just as you deceived me, by pretending that you were entertaining her husband to conversation in the parlour, while she was laboriously cooking you and me a fine meal. When, in fact, you and he were entertaining *each other*, in a somewhat different manner, in the larder. Deplorable behaviour, Watson! And now I must give *you* advice, my dear friend. Whatever the pain it may cause, to Hudson and to you, your relationship must cease immediately. Certainly no further meetings can occur in this house – I forbid that, absolutely. Even your lover would seem to have found the larder an inadequate location, and to have been advocating another – possibly your surgery? But surely I do not need to tell you what tumult and destruction any continuation of the relationship is likely to cause, for the entire Hudson family, as well as for your wife and yourself. If you and Hudson decide not to end your love-affair, all responsibility for the ultimate consequences – including destruction of the friendship between you and me – must be yours."

"'The friendship between you and me'! But that is a major cause of this affair, Holmes! You must be aware – surely you are aware – of my love for you. I have always loved you. Whatever dogs-body work you have asked of me; whatever service I could perform for you; whatever sneers or rejection I have sensed, at times, in our conversations; whatever spectacle I have made of myself in the eyes of others, as I follow your commands like the most menial servant – It is all because of my love for you; because I cannot bear to be parted from you for any length of time. Holmes! Please, I beg of you –"

I move spasmodically towards him, holding out my hands, yearning to take him in my arms. But he turns away abruptly. "Watson, control yourself. Do not make a fool of yourself. Sit down until you recover, then wash your face."

I am ashamed to say that, like Mrs Hudson earlier, I burst into tears. I stand in his study, and weep, while he watches me. Eventually,

I mutter, shakily, "I must go home. Ethel will be waiting for me. Will you – ?"

"I will follow you in an hour or so, Watson. Please tell your wife that I am very grateful for your invitation, and that I trust it does not inconvenience her to entertain me so unexpectedly for dinner. Tomorrow, with Mrs Hudson's return, all will be well again in these rooms. We will be back to normal."

As I make my way unsteadily down the stairs to his front door, high thin sounds begin to emanate from Holmes' violin as it is caressed by his bow.

This story, published here for the first time, was found among Dr Watson's papers after his death. At first, his family refused permission for its publication, arguing that its style and content are inferior to his earlier, well-known and greatly-admired stories, and that its author would not have wished it to be published. However, it can be argued that its style shows, in fact, a late experimental impulse of its author (note, for instance, the surely-deliberately-awkward first paragraph, and his striking use of the present-tense throughout), and that the story itself is very significant in other ways, especially in providing information hitherto unknown about the relationship between Sherlock Holmes and Dr Watson.

Russian Roulette

A note for the Reader:
The following two letters, written by Pyotr Ilyich Tchaikovsky's nephew 'Bob' Davidov to his Uncle Modest, the composer's brother, have been very loosely translated into English by myself. The letters came into my possession when my Great-Aunt Galina in New York, having been informed by her Doctor that she had pancreatic cancer and only a short while to live, summoned me to her bedside. Handing me a small wooden box, she told me that it contained two very important letters that had been given to a member of her Mother's family (by whom she did not know), many years earlier, and had been brought to North America when family-members escaped Russia in 1917. Now she wished me to accept and treasure the letters. "I have few relations in this country, and you are the only one I like and trust; also the only one who has learnt Russian, and values Russian culture," she said; "so I entrust these letters to you. You will see how significant they are." Of course I accepted her gift. However, I have decided not to keep the letters any longer; perhaps I am too superstitious, but I sense that they may be cursed. By the time you read this transcription, the originals will have been destroyed. Having considered them carefully, I am convinced that they are genuine. However, you, the critical reader, must decide whether to trust what they contain. Certainly the great composer's biographers will need to evaluate this text, since it resolves the debate over what has long been the most contentious event in Tchaikovsky's life: the nature and cause of his death. –PT

Klin: 25th October, 1906

My dear Uncle:

I know that you will be in the same state of anguish as I am today: for it is again the anniversary of his death. Thirteen years since Uncle Peter died! Neither of us can ever find release from that dreadful event. We have often talked of that. Our efforts to create a noble shrine to his memory – here in his house, which you bought from Alexey Sofronov so as to continue what he had begun, collecting together Uncle Peter's possessions where he was mostly so happy – must have been in part an attempt to deal with our pain. I wonder if that has truly helped you. I must confess now that it has not helped me.

Perhaps I was wrong to terminate my military career in 1897, as you argued when you tried to dissuade me; but at that time, four years after his death, I was so often maddened by grief that I knew I could never be an efficient officer. Yet since then all my attempts to follow him and become an artist, in music or poetry, have only mocked me with failure.

Why can I never find peace now? Yes, I loved him, deeply, and he loved me; even though I disappointed him. Should not memories of our love fill me with rejoicing rather than this eternal, disabling pain? I know these are questions that you cannot answer, and I do not seek to torment you with them as I torment myself. I feel so useless, and of course that feeds my despair.

Music! His music. Everywhere one hears it. Russia's greatest composer! At times I long to escape into an utter silence, unbroken by a single note of his music. Yet also I am drawn ineluctably towards any concert where his music is performed, and I sing his songs and play his piano pieces at midnight when I cannot sleep – which is almost every night. Even vodka does not help much now.

Recently I went to a concert featuring his Sixth Symphony, which you persuaded him to call the "Pathetique", and of course I was reminded that he dedicated it to me. Why? As his music died away into whispers of sorrow and suffering, I longed to ask him that again. Why did he do that? Why me? Was it intended as a message? Did that symphony symbolize his life? Or was it a prediction of *my* life after he was gone? Did he think of me at all as he composed it? He once told me that its meaning was his secret. It is still his secret!

I know that you cannot answer those questions, Uncle, any more than I can. He was so many personalities wrapped inside his one lovable, enigmatic being. He could be as imperious as the Tsar, he could be as gentle as a nursing mother, he could be as quick and subtle as a snake, he could be as considerate and gentle as a devoted servant like Alexey Sofronov, he could play silly jokes like a clown, he could be as loving as – oh, when he was in that mood, he *was* love, love incarnate. He was also childlike, both giving and demanding love as a small child does.

Do you remember how once, when I was a boy, he and I wrote letters to Anna Petrovna, at his instigation, informing her that he was dead – that he had shot himself? That became a family joke, but it could have been cruel to her, except that, as we knew would be the case, she was too phlegmatic to take the letters at all seriously. It could also have been a prediction.

Oh, these memories! I also recall vividly how he actually apologized to me from his sickbed for causing inconvenience! "You will lose respect for me after seeing these unpleasant things" he said with a smile, that unforgettably sweet smile. And those five days were so truly horrible, horrible – watching his suffering so helplessly. I would like to forget; but I cannot forget.

When he died I was twenty-one. Now I am thirty-four. Yet I am more confused – much more confused – than I was then, as a young man. At least I did not then question who I was. Who am I, Uncle? Another unanswerable question.

Somehow I knew, before he made me his favourite companion, that Uncle Peter was homosexual; it was whispered within the family, especially after he had married and then run away from his wife – I was a small boy then. But, as I honestly told you, he never once tried to make love to me – even when I would have welcomed it, if only to find out how it was for men being with other men. You said he became obsessive about my company, and when he was in America he wrote that every day away from me was "a day of torture". Of course I was flattered, and tried to respond, though his letters made me uncomfortable because I knew I could never express and return love as fully as he gave his love to me. Yet when we were actually together, he made no advances, and I was too shy to, however much I longed for his touch. He once said "You are too good for sex, Bob; our love means too much to me; when I need sex, I get it from others." Which others? Certainly Alexey Sofronov, his beloved Aleysha: you could have sex with a servant because he was of a lower class and without power – that's the only way I can understand it. I know of course that he was not just *any* servant; he was Uncle's valet for so long, and was such a fine man, although illiterate, that he had become a close friend and confidant. Still, he was a servant, and once I was bold enough to ask him if Uncle Peter ever made love to him. He looked embarrassed, and muttered that it was always his privilege to please the Master.

But it is getting late and the candle is burning low.

Dear Uncle, I beg you to reply as soon as you receive this letter. I need to talk to you. Please come. It is very important. Please do not fear that I will talk only about myself, and about my relationship with Uncle Peter, as I know I have been prone to do lately. I shall be here for four more days. I do not go out at all, even for walks. The servants see to all my necessities. I read and write, and I sing and play the piano – his piano. I am lonely, very lonely. Please reply. Please come.

Your loving Nephew
Bob

Klin: 29th October, 1906

My dear Uncle:

No reply to my letter has come. You have not come. I feel desolate. I fear you have abandoned me – you too. Everything is meaningless. I cannot endure this much longer. In fact, I am ready to end it. When you receive this letter, I will probably be dead. "Russian Roulette": a matter of luck, but I have no luck, I never did have luck, and the bullet awaits me.

I have been singing and playing Uncle Peter's last songs, the ones he composed very near the end of his life. I think they were his final compositions, and perhaps they are his greatest music. You remember that in my last letter I was wondering what message he might have intended in his Sixth Symphony, the "Pathetique"? The message in these songs is very clear to me. They are about loneliness, sadness and death. They say collectively "My time has come – it is my time to die." Let me quote from some of the poems, sent to him, as no doubt you know, by the poet called Danil Rathaus: '... alone as before, I expect nothing of the years to come ... sorrow presses down on my breast with strange power ...'. The last one begins 'Once more I am all alone, once more filled with pain' and ends 'Friend! Pray for me – I pray for you'. The piano repeats long slow chords, a bell tolling. Why did he set those words to music? He once told me, with tears in his eyes, about the mysterious Stranger who commissioned the dying Mozart to compose a Requiem. Was Danil Rathaus his Stranger? I think these six songs – yes, again the number six! – are his Requiem. Do you remember that I told you he said to me, just after he had finished composing the Sixth Symphony, and just before he composed those six songs, that it was his "Requiem"? He was always meditating on Death, I think, at that time.

Suicide. We both know that Uncle Peter had attempted suicide earlier in his life, and that he often spoke about committing suicide, when he was depressed – and he was often depressed. We also know – we do, Uncle – that his death was suicide, just as mine will be. Yet we have participated in an elaborate hoax – you, the doctors, I, and a host of others – to conceal the actuality and "protect his reputation". As if suicide were a disgrace rather than the obvious solution to an intensely painful situation, one impossible to endure any longer! When life becomes too painful to entertain, death becomes a welcome guest.

Uncle Peter was ill long before his death, with those recurring bouts of stomach pain. He was also depressed in 1893, especially after that stupid "Court of Honor". I think he realized that it was an elaborate joke – a cruel one, like some of his own jokes – set up by those old fellow-students of his at the School of Jurisprudence who were jealous of his fame and eminence. But, as you know, he had always been extremely sensitive about his homosexuality, believing it to be a moral failing that he should have been able to overcome – and especially he always dreaded its becoming a matter of wide public knowledge. So he was in a mood, as I am now, to invoke and challenge Fate by playing 'Russian Roulette'. That is why he chose to drink a whole glass of unboiled water in the Leiner Restaurant that night, after the theater – knowing very well the danger of contracting cholera. In fact, he refused to wait for boiled water and went into the kitchen for the fatal glass of unboiled water; I saw that, and I think he knew that I saw it. So Russian, is it not? Suicide, which we pretend not to acknowledge – always requiring Fate to make the final decision. And I am recalling at this moment Uncle Peter telling me that, in his early years, he composed an Overture, or it may have been a 'symphonic poem', dedicated to Fate. He said he had always been fascinated by Fate.

And Fate accepted his invitation that very night, when he began to suffer the first of the dreadful consequences: nausea, vomiting, diarrhoea. Fate had answered by sending him what he had invoked: cholera, the most painful of deaths. I was so angry with him for that, but also consumed with sorrow and pity, as his intense suffering began. To be beside him to the end, talking and smiling, holding his hand, was what I knew he would wish of me. But, as I have said, it was dreadful, monstrous, every moment of watching and feeling that appalling misery. You know how it was, even though we avoided talking about it afterwards. You were there. You were often there. When the end came, we were both at his bedside, and he gazed intensely at us – I see his eyes now – gazing, gazing into our souls until the death rattle began.

That's how it was, Uncle. It was suicide. "Russian Roulette". Suicide. We must accept that. I cannot any longer tolerate the story that the cholera which killed him was mere chance. He *wanted* to die then, Uncle. He asked for death. Perhaps he judged that his task was done; perhaps he was utterly exhausted, worn out; perhaps he believed again, with extreme conviction, that his musical creativity was waning – how can we know? What I do know is that those weeks of his illness, death and funeral were a nightmare beyond all endurance. Yet somehow I have endured, until now.

Uncle Peter was life and death to me. His friendship and love gave me inexpressible joy, even though I could never satisfy his own need – and sometimes, I am ashamed to say, resented it as demanding too much from me. But I am sad, now, that I disappointed him so often. I have just re-read his letters to me, for the last time. Do you know, he even threatened to withdraw the dedication of the Sixth Symphony to me if I did not show more "interest" in him! Yet I felt so fortunate, so privileged, to be his nephew, to be near him while he poured out such a glory of music for Russia and the world. Did he never guess how much I loved and admired him? How much I was in awe of him? He was, he is, incomparable. Yet his genius overwhelmed me. In its shadow I could only feel incompetent, useless, untalented, uninspired – a failure, a failure. All the affection he lavished on me could not alter that. I wonder if he ever sensed my agony? Perhaps he did, but could not help me. And then he went.

My confusion is total. I wanted to be homosexual because he was, but even now I don't know if I am – I have had sex with both men and women, not infrequently, and found no absolute difference, in pleasure or pain. So I have recoiled from both. I rely on self-pleasuring when the need comes. That seems sufficient now. I have retreated from all relationships. I have retreated from myself.

So I depart, Uncle. I would like to be buried near Uncle Peter, if that is possible. Soon Russia will change radically. I feel that, I know that. In fact, the change is already beginning. To be aware of it, one has only to pay attention. Soon it will no longer be possible for members of the upper class to use those of the lower class in whatever ways we wish, as even Uncle Peter did. There will no longer be classes. We will all be brothers. That is my vision and my hope. But, however much Russia and the wide world change, I know that Uncle

Peter's music will survive, and go on giving joy to multitudes as long as humans exist. To use Alexey Sofronov's words, it was my privilege to know him intimately, and to try to give him whatever pleasure I could.

I thank you for all your kindness and all your generosity, my dear Uncle. May your remaining days be serene. Pray for me – I pray for you.

Your loving Nephew,
Bob

The House of Renning

Stratford, Ontario
8 August 2006

Dear Rupert:

I hesitated over the "Dear", then decided that it is merely the conventional way of beginning a letter and that it need not signify affection. As you would expect, no affection is implied in this case; though, as we are twin brothers, perhaps it should suggest an underlying regret that affection has dwindled to absence, to impossibility. Surely there was affection between us once? When we were small boys, before Mother died – yes, I think so. But that is so long ago, and so many unforgivable things have been done and said since then, alas.

However, this letter, my last to you, must not sink into that morass of past emotion. It is to be concerned with the present, the recent past, and the immediate future. It is to be concerned especially with the disposal of Renning House and its environs – the whole Estate; which of course is our joint responsibility. That will raise other matters: so I must also deal, briefly, with two intransigent personalities, namely ourselves; and, also briefly, I hope, with Grandfather, Father, and our family history.

The property matter can be stated simply and incontrovertibly. I do not wish to leave you in any doubt whatever about my views and wishes, Rupert. I have made certain arrangements with my Lawyer (with whose name and address you are familiar), and you may contact him at any time after reading this – if indeed he has not contacted you first. I shall be sending him a copy of this letter. I have thought to leave the entire matter of Renning House for lawyers to work out (but you of course are a lawyer, and I assume that, as in the past, you will prefer to handle your side of the matter yourself, so I must take that into account); also I decided that I owe it to our forebears (especially Father and Grandfather), and to both of us, to compose a personal written statement, my Last Will and Testament, so to speak. I trust it will at least be granted a respectful hearing. (And I trust you will be able to read it: my scrawl was always a liability – and letters in longhand are such a rarity, now that E-mails and faxes and, what are they, Blackberries, have come to dominate communication.)

Here goes.

1. I feel strongly that Renning House should be left to the People of Ontario (you and Marcus will both know how best to accomplish that). Neither of us has heirs; our only family connections are distant, at best; since Wayne died, I have no close friend to care about, and I doubt that you have ever had a close friend. On the other hand, the house, and the family that built it and lived in it for two centuries, are significant in the history of Ontario. We disagreed (as we have disagreed on every topic, it seems) about the House's intrinsic architectural merit – I will have more to say about the interior renovation of 1971, that painful topic, later in this letter – but I believe the House and its contents, and the whole Estate, must be kept intact, as far as possible: surely you will accept that? Then there are the Family Papers, which, I have been assured, are of considerable historical importance. They must be preserved for posterity of course, and should be held *in situ*, under an arrangement that stipulates their being professionally sorted and catalogued. That in itself will require the resources of the Ontario Government. In fact, Renning House must be declared a Historical Site, and I trust it will be. You have been a major political and financial supporter of the Party now in power – surely that should carry weight with the Premier; and I am still well-known in Ontario, I think, as an actor, playwright and, latterly, "television personality".

I am glad that there can be no question of our getting together to discuss these matters, even if, as I suspect, there is a measure of agreement about fundamentals. (That would certainly disappear in a trice if we did meet!) However, if you disregard or repudiate any of my wishes, I have requested Marcus to appeal to the Premier and Cabinet on my behalf. I believe they would respond positively, if only in view of the known historical and architectural significance of Renning House. But I also believe that such a procedure will not be necessary, and that your instinct for self-justification and self-promotion will ensure that you recognise the very negative effects of a public family dispute.

2. So much for the matter of the future of Renning House. It seems strange to be focussed on the future of a house when my own future is almost non-existent! But then that merely underlines what I have been writing: that the family is what matters, our forebears; and where they settled and built and lived their productive lives; their contribution to the development of this great country. (An old-fashioned point of view, perhaps, as immigrants from many different lands and cultures now flood into our cities; but one that matters, I believe, even to those immigrants – who will do their part, one hopes, in the noble enterprise that is Canada.)

Great-great-Grandfather Alexander was an amazingly energetic man: how did he accomplish so much – clearing the land, taming the river, establishing his mill, organizing and leading other pioneers as they built a village that grew into a town (but never into a city, and, as you know, long gone except for what is now the gatehouse)? I must not turn this into a history lesson. Let me just summarise: the next two Renning patriarchs, Arthur and Alexander II, continued the family's upward progress, entering local governance; and our Grandfather, Matthew, was elected a Member of Parliament, and, in the aftermath of the Great War and his distinguished service in it, became Minister of Agriculture for two years. But oh, that War. Ours wasn't the only Canadian family wrecked by it, doing our duty by the Empire; but the wreckage we suffered was extreme, extending right into the present, and ultimately destroying the family. (You may not agree with this interpretation: I know you have no patience with my near-pacifism – Brennan let drop you said that to him once.) (By the way, I trust that Brennan will be awarded a substantial pension if his services as Estate Manager become supererogatory: in my observation and experience, when I was in and out of residence in the House during the 1960s and early 1970s, he was always efficient, dedicated, and, moreover, very pleasant company.)

The War. You know what it did to Father, poor man, physically and mentally; and even Grandfather the Colonel, for all his military bearing and values, was severely affected. No need to run through all the pain and deprivation that the so-called Great War brought us. And Mama was little help, to Father or us. Did you ever wonder how they could bring themselves to call us, twin boys who were anyway faced with the difficulty of defining ourselves, Rupert and Robert! (which were not even family names!). But that was a peccadillo at most; it was Dad's physical suffering, the lost leg and gas-ruined lungs, not to speak of his Shell-Shock (now of course renamed Post-Traumatic Stress Disorder), his periods of silence and withdrawal, his sudden rages – Poor Mother! No wonder she died not very long after he did. I cannot now blame Father (though I did when younger), but in those days suicide implied severe moral failing. You will remember, as I do, that Grandfather would never speak about the War after Father's suicide, and mentioned his son only if forced to. One can only imagine his reaction to the responsibility of bringing up two small boys (he was 71 when Mama died in 1942), but I think he did well by us, despite his rather fierce manner, and of course with the assistance of Aunt Phyllis and Miss Major until we were packed off to boarding school in Toronto.

I know I am treading over territory familiar to you, Rupert, but I'm trying to piece it all together, to understand our disaster, one last time. So bear with me!

3. Now I must also inform you that a historian and biographer, one Raymond Cartwright, of McMaster University in Hamilton, has been in touch with me during the past few months, and may already have contacted you – I put him in touch with Marcus, who has approved of his research and has assured me that he will keep an

eye on it. Cartwright's project, as he calls it, is a biography of yours truly. I tried to dissuade him, but he was adamant that Canada and the world need a record of my life and "dramatic achievements, especially at Stratford"! The best I have been able to do is sketch our family history for him and urge him to include his study of it in the biography, preferably as more than background. I understand that he should not need your formal approval for any of this, since you and I are in joint and equal control of Renning House and its contents; but I have provided him, through Marcus, with a document that will ensure his right to investigate the Family Papers and also make it possible for him to interview staff (like Brennan) and neighbours as well as my friends and colleagues, and whatever family he can locate and persuade. I told him I would inform you about his project, and of course he would greatly appreciate your co-operation and support.

4. Not much more! Courage. I come to the recent past and the present.

Now it becomes tricky, in view of our infamous confrontation of 1971. Why my renovation of the servants' quarters to provide a comfortable residence for James and myself should have been, as you so surprisingly termed it, the "final straw", I have never fully understood. My main memory of the episode is of you, red-faced and shaking like a leaf, screaming imprecations and slamming doors: I feared you were about to have a heart-attack, so, remembering Mama's, I gave way to your tantrum. James never forgave me for that, and his departure, followed closely by mine, from what I had planned as the retreat both of us needed, was immediate and final. If I could forgive you for everything else, I could never forgive you for that. And who did you think you were, behaving like some avenging crone? You had shown no interest in Renning House for many many years, while you were climbing legal ladders to the ultimate glory of High Court Judge. (You a Judge!) It was Marcus who, ten years ago, told me you had had no legal right to turn me out of our home. Moreover the renovations were minimal and reversible, in the House itself; and, in the servants' quarters, which had anyway been added to the back of the House by Great-Grandfather, all I'd done was to create a bedroom suite and a bathroom with shower. (What actually brought you to Renning House – with two policemen! – that morning was a malicious neighbour's false report, prompted by homophobia, and no doubt the fact that James was Black. I learned that from Brennan later; he and I corresponded fitfully for several years.) Your behaviour was outrageous, Rupert, and mine pusillanimous; the result being a rift that could never be healed.

I hated our famous college with a passion, and left it ill-educated and determined to confront the upper class of Ontario in whatever way possible: whereas you had gathered round you a sycophantic set of its scions. I was bullied and abused (even now I can't bring myself to recall some incidents): you sucked up to them, the teachers and housemasters and prefects, and had your reward of effusive approval and acclamatory academic recommendation. (No, enough. I will not allow myself to be bitter as all this ends. I took the road less travelled by – and eventually it led to some pleasure and considerable achievement, though of course not the sort of achievement you ever valued.) What strikes me now is how very far apart we had grown, in every way, by the time we left high-school. Our divergent paths were set in stone. You went on to the University of Toronto and Oxford (Rhodes Scholar, of course) and Osgoode; and I to wander the western world (ever the Playboy I!). We ignored each other, and in those years only Grandfather's persistent letters linked us to Renning House and, indirectly, each other.

5. And now I come to a crux, perhaps *the* crux. Much of what follows may be new to you. My acting and playwrighting career came about by chance, in England: I was all but penniless and on the point of ignoring my pride to telegraph Grandfather for more money, when a middle-aged man I met in a pub, impressed by my voice and "charisma" (he said), suggested I audition for a part at Stratford-upon-Avon. Which I did, since the theatre was a bus-ride away.

I was asked to read a speech by Hamlet, most unsuitably, and, to my amazed delight, was taken on as an extra. But there was more to that than luck, as I soon discovered when I was summoned to the Director's office. I won't tell you what happened between us: it matters now only for the consequences. Yes, I was a pretty young man, and yes, the Director was homosexual, and the middle-aged man was his stage-manager. Some of my more painful college experiences now came in useful and, more importantly, I realised that I *liked* the gay theatrical life I was now entering. I had a series of love-affairs, mainly with beautiful leading-men since they were the elite, and expected their talents to be rewarded with frequent dalliances. (I'm still holding back – why? I *want* to shock you. So for "dalliances" read "fucks".) That was *my* ladder to success – though I hasten to add that, like you, I do have thespian talents. And I soaked up advice from successful elders (I vividly recall being told by one, Larry I think, "Always make sure your first entrance is unforgettable, my boy", excellent advice) and soon I was becoming known as a "promising newcomer", playing roles like Mercutio and Laertes, acclaimed by critics, definitely on my way to English (and potentially international) stardom.

But Canada called me back, in the ironic form of James, who, though English, had been offered several major roles at Stratford Ontario, notably as Othello, and wanted me acting opposite him as his Iago (he also, I add immodestly, wanted me as Me). So there I was, back near home – actually within a few miles of Renning House, which is why it seemed not merely convenient but sensible for James and I to live there when we could, away from the passions and back-biting and tensions characteristic of any theatre-centred society. (After 1971 I never went back, never saw the House or Estate again; I had sworn as I left it, with your shrieks in my ears, that I would never return; and that promise, unlike so many others, I have kept. Are you glad to know you instilled a modicum of integrity into me?) Thereafter, my theatrical rise was dizzying; the fury you had provoked morphed into energy, and ruthless egotistical ambition, and on the stage flared into a blaze of brilliance (I'm semi-quoting enemies and friends here). (Poor James: I ripped him apart, Iago rampant, Othello totally subservient – I can still see the hurt bewilderment in his eyes as his confidence seeped away.) After two seasons I was the major "draw", the Lion of Stratford Ont (you must have been, however reluctantly, aware of that): the critics adored me, Americans clamoured over the border for me, young actors threw themselves at me. In fact, my life became too much for me. Drink and drugs, so easily available, began to destroy me from within; gradually lethargy and boredom undermined ambition; pleasure-seeking became my only consistent value, even though the pleasure was diminished by guilt and loneliness. (I am trying to be honest. Yes, I *was* lonely, so lonely.) That's when Dorothy entered my life, and saved me.

6. I don't think you even knew that we had met, Dorothy and I – she said she'd never tell you, and if ever there was an honest person, it was Dee. We became friends. Your wife and I were friends! Not only did you, quite unintentionally, give me fame and fortune as an actor, by kicking me out of my home, but you saved my career, just as unintentionally, through your wife! I was in New Zealand last year when I learned that she had died in an accident, and I was so devastated that I considered flying back for the funeral; but it wouldn't have been possible (the news was a few days old), and she would not have wanted that, if only to save you from any awkwardness in a public situation (I saw a news-photo in which you, as noble "grieving husband", were flanked by what looked like the whole panoply of minor legal and political and diplomatic Ottawa royalty). What a woman Dee was! I could write so much about her qualities, and our times together – our conversations, the laughter, the fun; but I don't think you would want to hear about that, and I'm not trying to torment you.

But perhaps I should tell you how we met. I was doing Macbeth (a part that exhausted me more than most) when I was handed a note, after a performance, reading "Please can we meet? Your admiring sister-in-law, D". To be honest, I was reluctant, fearing any connection with her would bring trouble from *you*. But I was also curious, and curiosity won out. She was beautiful, vivid, warm, open, the best sort of American woman. We had a drink together on that first occasion, and our conversation commenced – to be continued, deepening and broadening, ever-enriching, on so many other occasions, always after performances, and usually over dinner. Sometimes Andy was there too – I liked him, I was even attracted to him, but he was devotedly heterosexual, totally committed to Dee; before she introduced him, she had told me that she was sometimes accompanied to the theatre by her "Mister" – "'Mister'?" I queried – "Oh, men have their Mistresses, why shouldn't women have their Misters?" – typical Dee, that, witty and open. (I wonder what has happened to Andy? Someone told me he was driving the car, but that may not have been so; *mea culpa*, I never thought to find out.) Always perceptive, Dee quickly saw how things were going with me, the decline towards alcoholism, the embarrassingly fumbled moments on stage. I was drowning – not waving. (Once I forgot my lines completely – even which part I was playing in which play – and nearly fell into the audience.) Quietly and efficiently, Dee pulled me back to the shore: I am eternally grateful to her.

Only once did we discuss her relationship with you, and not in detail – she was rightly reticent about that. She respected you, she said – you were principled and hard-working, a valuable and necessary authority in society. Your marriage was essentially contractual – her main duty was to be beside you on all appropriate public occasions, to be hostess when needed, to smile fondly, to dress fashionably. She found you cold and distant in private, but that was an acceptable price for her pampered situation ("I enjoy being pampered" she once said – "That's the American in me, I guess"); neither of you wanted children, she said. I asked only one question: "Do you think Rupert is gay?" – "Of course he is. Seeing him look at Andy when he thinks I won't notice, that's a total giveaway. He is also very careful, fastidious – I don't think he ever has sex, except occasional masturbation – perhaps he's even a virgin. He must have learned how to stay closeted at an early age." (Yes, I could have commented, he did; as a schoolboy, or even earlier.) "You and your brother seem to be so different, opposites in every way," she went on, "but you're also very alike. That's why I was so intrigued to meet you – when I found out, somehow, that you were twins, and Rupert would not talk about you, didn't even want to acknowledge your existence. But twins can never escape each other, I think."

There you have it. Dee's wisdom. We are prisoners of each other, you and I. You will cavil, I know. That also is usual, I fear. Originality is impossible. We are only humans! Twins are humans, Rupert. We have been moving through our lives predictably, side by side, whether we like that or not. But you seem to have missed so much fun; the pleasure that good sex gives, evanescent but indescribably intense; and the longer, deeper joy of close, loving relationships – companionship, friendship. The compensations for being Human! I don't regret any of that. It was a gift, a privilege.

7. So I am ending where I started – where we both started. With the personal. We are the last members of a once-great family, and, for all our varied individual achievements, we are pitifully impotent. Our family ends here, and now. And why should that matter? But Renning House remains, a shell perhaps – no, not a shell, an empty container from which all life has evaporated; but a cornucopia out of which the future will blossom – no, no, no, I deceive myself, don't I? Of course I have no way of knowing. None at all. Others will decide, when we two are long gone. That big beautiful House squatting so ostentatiously beside the fecund fields and rolling river that made it possible – What will become of it?

Goodbye, Rupert. (I apologise for writing more than I intended – far too much; I guess I was always garrulous.) I wish you a good death. I do forgive you; I must. Forgive me.

Your twin brother, Robert

cc Marcus Holloway; Raymond Cartwright

A Long Farewell

Simon, I have just received a letter from your brother. He tells me that you have died (almost exactly a week ago, apparently), "surrounded by your loving family", and that you have been "interred" beside your parents and other family members. (Presumably in that mausoleum on your family estate that you once described to me.) It's a short letter – a note, really – as befits their low opinion of me. "We thought you might like to know," it ends ("might"!). No openly nasty comments this time – for that, at least, I guess I must be grateful.

But Simon – My lovely and beloved Simon, how can I ever find closure? When I can never begin to forget you – or the dreadful way we were separated, after those joyful years together. I have been so angry, my dear. Perhaps you know that now, in your purified Being. And know also that, with the support of my religious belief, the anger is gone; I am calm again. (I do believe in the After Life, you will recall; I always did; even after all our arguments on that and other religious topics – our "friendly disputes" – I can only hope I am right, and that you are now resting and rejoicing, transformed into your Ultimate State. And that I will join you before long, so we can express our love for each other in utter joy, for all Eternity.)

Last month I told Deborah, my lawyer, that I don't wish to proceed with the case against your family for taking you away like that. She was disappointed, saying it might have set an important precedent for the rights of people with Alzheimer's, and even the rights of older homosexual men – the publicity alone would have been valuable, she said, however the case turned out. But I told her I couldn't face any more dissension and turmoil. You and I always wanted peace in our personal lives – peace to be able to live in love together, so I think you would approve of my decision.

As I told your Sister when she came to see us last October (before she stole you away), I could not understand (and still cannot understand) why your family would never accept the fact of our loving relationship, our total commitment to each other. I remember how unpleasant they were to me (even your Mother – I never told you, but she called me a pervert, and a thief – and said that if I didn't "set you free" she would never talk to either of us again!). I think now that perhaps, to some extent anyway, her behaviour was caused by the double shock – triple shock – of your announcing that you were gay, introducing me as your lover, and telling them that you would be leaving in a few days to live with me in Canada. I didn't sympathise with them at the time, but I guess I've come to understand how hard it was for your parents' generation to deal with all that. And you thought they even suspected I was after the family name and fortune, being a lowly Canadian!

I know you said it was necessary, for various reasons, to face them openly and sternly, and immediately, but I wished then, and I wish now, it had all been different; then perhaps there would have been the chance of a positive relationship with all your family (your sister was kind then, at first, wasn't she? – and always wrote you, and sent birthday and Christmas cards). Of course, when I met you, I didn't know how important your family is in English society, and you always said "Not as important as they bloody think they are" – but I was so taken aback to find I was in love with the younger son of an Earl – all those famous names and a family history going back to the Norman Conquest! Only I do think that, if they had truly loved you, they would have made efforts to accept me eventually – during our twenty-four years together. (I guess they always hoped our relationship wouldn't last?) And now it's too late.

And what a pity it is that they didn't get to appreciate your achievements as an artist, my dear. "The best landscape-painter in Canada today" and all those awards and wonderful reviews. No, I won't say any more about that – you didn't like me to sing your praises; you were always much too humble, my dear! And those three wonderful exhibitions in Montreal, Toronto and Vancouver. My only useful talents were as your manager, publicist and companion; but when we were together, when we worked together, "wot larks, wot larks, wot larks"! Yes, we were a great partnership in every way. Of course, I'm sure your family would have been proud of you if you'd made your reputation in England – but in the Colonies – ! Enough of that; it was their loss. And nothing and nobody could separate us (yes, we both had affairs – every man you ever met wanted you! – but we were honest with each other, and always forgave each other, and we always found our way back together – never were emotionally or spiritually separated for long).

My dear, my beloved, I must stop this. "No tears, no tears, buck up!" – I can hear you saying that. But it's hard not to weep about the Alzheimer's. "Early onset," they said (after you began to lose your memory and couldn't paint as you used to – though some critics admired your "new style"). "No cure," they said. "Should consider putting him into a home," they said (but I would never do that; of course I wouldn't; and I was in a position to retire from my job and look after you, so I did). But it was so unfair! To see you lose your alert humorous ways, your sharp focus, your intelligence and wit, your happiness, your ability to recall our life together – recall even who I was. (Not just my name, my very being.) But I do *not* believe that you lost your personality, deep down; you were still Simon, the Simon I loved for twenty-seven years and will always love.

And then your family – How could they do that? I had to tell them, after the diagnosis (or I thought I had to – perhaps I should have kept quiet). At first they refused to believe it; your Brother, the Earl (he had just succeeded your Father), seemed to think it was a plot of some sort ("There is nothing in our Family that might suggest a propensity for dementia"!), and then wrote to say the Family were all "extremely concerned" about your situation (the hurtful insinuation being, of course, that I wasn't looking after you properly). Then your Sister wrote to say she'd like to visit; I was delighted and said so. But I didn't for one moment suspect a plot to take you from me! Apparently your Mother had said "I must see Simon before I die", so your Brother made the arrangements, including another passport for you (I guess you can do that sort of thing in England if you're an Earl).

I have found it hard to forgive Sheila for her part in all this. She told me, after being with us for a week, that she was very impressed by the care I was giving you, and could see how much I loved you – but I should watch my health, and be careful, for your sake as well as mine, not to wear myself out; and she suggested that I take advantage of her visit to spend some time with my Mother, who was ill (she died two months before you, of cancer; of course you never knew that – oh, how she loved you, Simon – and how you loved her, and how I miss you both – so much, so much, so much).

So I left you for four days. And when I got back – the house was empty. Not even a note to tell me where you were. I was in a panic, of course, and imagined all sorts of explanations, none of them at all consoling – I went to the Police, and they contacted your Brother, who told them Sheila had found me abusing you, and had taken you back to England, where you were living "very happily surrounded by your loving Family" and were "now receiving good medical care". Of course I was devastated. I tried to speak to Sheila, and even your Brother, but both of them refused – twice he slammed the phone down right in my ear. I wrote letters then – but no response. Silence.

Well, why am I writing all this? To clear my mind a little, perhaps. To get rid of the last vestiges of resentment and anger? To express some of the pain I've been feeling? But I do also feel that in some way, mysterious but real, I am in contact with you, my dear, communicating with you. Enough now. Let me just finish this, then I will "shut up", my dear (as you often suggested when I began "fulminating"!), and after that I'll try not to say any more about us, to anyone, ever –

I was advised to get a lawyer, and she agreed to take on my case, but warned me after consulting British and Canadian Law that we would have to prove you had been transported from Canada to England against your will – but how could we do that, with your Alzheimer's making it impossible for you even to remember what had happened? You see – impossible. And now not relevant – at least, not for the two of us. (Surely nothing like it will happen to anyone else?)

Oh, I guess I could have begged them to let me see you. I thought of that – I'd have flown over in a flash. But I knew they wouldn't. After all, we weren't married, you and I, we couldn't be at that time – so your family owned you.

Perhaps it never was relevant for us, my dear – conflict with your family, and its inevitably negative effects. (Thank goodness, they have said nothing about your paintings – probably because they could take no pleasure in Newfoundland landscapes; I intend to donate them to the National Gallery, and galleries here, where they deserve to be, loved and appreciated.) So what *is* relevant now? That we loved each other. Your body (which gave us both so much pleasure) has been buried in your family's cemetery, near your father and forefathers. They have welcomed you back, now that you are dead. They are reconciled to you. Your mother was able to see her son after a quarter century, and now can die content. All is forgiven, perhaps. But do I truly forgive *them*? – I must try, I will try.

I will never forget the last time I saw you (though of course I had no suspicion that it *would* be the last time). I hugged you and kissed you goodbye, in the kitchen – And as I reversed the car down the driveway, I looked up, and you were standing at the window, gazing out, as if in the midst of painting another glorious view. I waved; you didn't wave back, but I think you smiled.

'Farewell, a last farewell, to all your greatness.'

I love you, Simon. Always, always, always. I love you. I love you.

Crass Casualty

To Whom It May Concern:

You will have found this document on the small table between the corpses of my beloved Companion of twelve years, Keith Owen Nash, and myself, Arnold James Holloway: he in our bed and I in a chair nearby. I hope that the Police will have acted quickly after receiving the letter I posted this afternoon, to reach them tomorrow morning: I am anxious that our neighbours, who have not harmed us in any way, should not be inconvenienced. (One has read stories in the Press about corpses being discovered, after many weeks or even months, because of the foul smell they were emitting.) I do apologize to all whose employment has involved them in the distressing physical consequences of our decision to depart: notably, the disposal of our corpses, and of our remaining furniture (I have disposed of our personal papers, books and other effects, including my collections of glass figurines and china dogs).

If only one could depart from this earth without the attendant physical mess! At least there will be no-one to mourn our passing, and therefore no need for a memorial service. In the drawer of the bedside table, you will find, under our Wills (with the name and telephone number of our Lawyer), documents relating to the cremation arrangement I set up last year. I have posted a letter (with a financial contribution) to the Reverend Angus McNeill of Christ Church, requesting him to offer prayers over our corpses, before or as they are cremated. (He will not remember me, I think, although he and I conversed briefly after the only service I attended at his church; he seemed to me a sincere and generous man.) (This house, and our financial savings, have been willed to charities; but I have appended a check for $2,000 to pay for the removal of our corpses and furniture, hoping that sum will suffice.)

You may ask, in resentment or perhaps even curiosity, why we have decided on an exit so unusual, and so burdensome to you. The succinct answer is that no other seemed possible. I have certainly struggled with our decision over the past two days, while preparing for today. However, after careful reconsideration, I came always to the same conclusion. Early in our relationship (I remember that it was soon after we began living together), Keith and I made a pact, to die together if one of us were doomed. It become impossible for me to discuss departure arrangements with him, of course; but I know he would wish me to honour our pact.

In mitigation, let me explain, briefly, the situation in which we have found ourselves. It has evolved (and intensified) over the past four years, following my early-retirement as a Teacher, that retirement being a consequence of Keith's descent into dementia. You see, someone had to care for him, and I was the only one who could. It has been both my duty and my pleasure. Keith and I have lived together, in great happiness and complete trust, for over a dozen years, ever since we met as lonely middle-aged homosexual men (he having recently lost his former companion to AIDS, I having recently lost my Mother). I thank God for Keith, and I bless the day that brought us together: we have celebrated that day, every year since; it was much more important to us than our birthdays, or Easter or Christmas.

Keith is older than me by nine years. He has a wonderful, gentle sense of humour: which was one of the qualities that attracted me to him. After we came to know each other, he would joke that I was attracted to old men because no young one would ever look at me! (There was some truth in that: I have always known I am physically unprepossessing, and in fact was quite surprised when he first paid attention to me. But we were "old men" then only according to the extreme homosexual standard: I was forty-five, he fifty-four.) We met by chance in a "gay bar", Woody's (during my third visit there); enjoyed conversing together; became intimate a month later; and married five years ago, just as soon as the new law came into force (I think we were the fifth couple to do so). It was a very small civil ceremony: neither of us had family, or close friends, and I am shy, especially in homosexual groups (no doubt as a consequence of being in the closet for so long).

You see, in a Catholic primary school, even now, you would risk losing your position if you "came out"; and it was far, far worse when I began my teaching career, thirty-three years ago. (A fellow teacher, whom I liked, was "fired"; without even any opportunity to respond to accusations, made by two of her students, that she had made lesbian overtures in the Gym.) It might have been slightly easier for Keith, as a Civil Servant, to "come out", if he had decided to; but he preferred to keep his sexuality secret. Some homosexual acquaintances whom we encountered at meetings of Prime Timers (after we joined that organization, during the past decade, when gradual social change was blunting homophobia in Ontario) made it clear that they considered those who had not "come out" much earlier in their lives to be cowardly and even dishonest; so Keith and I again retreated, abandoning our desire to find friends in the gay community of Toronto.

Looking back, I think we made the wrong decision. However, it was also owing, not only to the fear of negative consequences if we identified ourselves too openly as homosexuals; but to the fear (even in the 1990s) that dominated most homosexual men: of AIDS, the plague destroying so many of them (as I wrote above, Keith had lost his previous partner, Ben, to AIDS). In short, there seemed to be wisdom, not only crass self-preservation, in keeping our relationship secret. For four years after our meeting, Keith and I maintained separate homes, many kilometers apart, meeting during the week only at concerts and in Woody's (mainly because we had first met there); and spent only weekends together (in his apartment or my house, alternately). What a narrow, paltry, life-denying arrangement that now seems; but so we lived, then, Keith and I, and were mostly very happy, whenever we were together.

Re-reading what I have so far written, I see that I *was* dishonest (thoughtlessly rather than intentionally) when I wrote that we had no family. The situation was, rather, that our families were no longer part of our lives. In Keith's case, that was because his Father threw him out of the family home when, at the age of sixteen, he told his parents that he was homosexual; he then came to Toronto from the small town he'd grown up in, and for several years lived with an unmarried Aunt who had earlier shown him love and acceptance. By the time he and I met, his parents were dead, and so was the Aunt, who had treated him, always, like a son (and whom he came to believe was lesbian). He told me that his siblings (it was apparently quite a large family) had repudiated him, under their Father's influence, so he had cut himself off from them; they were, no doubt, ashamed to have a homosexual brother, and he had been bitterly disappointed by their rejection. (About five years ago, one of his sisters contacted Keith, by telephone, but he told her it was too late for any reconciliation.)

In my case, I did not admit, even to myself, that I was homosexual, until my Mother, noting that I had never shown any interest in girls, wondered, gently, if I was "queer". What a relief! I remember weeping on her shoulder that night, even though I was then twenty-two, and a student at teachers' college (I was living at home then, as earlier, when I was at university; I participated little in student life; but earned a very good B.A. Hons. degree and teaching qualification). My Mother also warned me that my Father, a deeply religious man, would have very great difficulty dealing with knowledge of my homosexuality, and that, if I ever behaved in a way that would identify me publicly as homosexual, I would be at risk of violent attack in the community (as well as, of course, bringing disgrace to the whole family). My Brother, five years older, was a very good hockey-player (he even tried out for the NHL), which made matters worse for me. (He died of a heart-attack four years ago; he had lived most of his life in Winnipeg, and clearly had no wish to reconnect with me.)

As we were a dutiful Catholic family, my Mother arranged for me to be counselled by a young priest whose sermons she admired. But he spoke to me coldly and severely, recommending self-control and regular Confession as antidotes to my "state of sin". I left the Church soon afterwards (to my Mother's distress), but have always retained a love for some Bible passages (especially Psalm 23, which offers so much comfort). Somehow my Father discovered that I was homosexual (I suspected the young priest as his informant, perhaps taking revenge for my apostasy, but that would have been very un-Christian of him, so I may well have been wrong; and I now see that he was probably as bewildered about sexuality as I was; and taking refuge in the Church's harsh values). My Father said nothing to me, but I could tell (from his even colder demeanour towards me) that he knew; and, when I asked her, my Mother confessed that he did know, but had said to her "We will not talk about it, now or ever. He has made his choice."

That is more than enough biographical information about Keith and me. I intended only to provide background information about us, but got carried away (as I tend to do when I write), and now I do not have time to reconsider and revise this text. Keith is still breathing, though very lightly now – his chest moves up and down almost imperceptibly. Soon I will recite our farewell service, which we adapted together from Keith's Anglican *Book of Common Prayer* (given to him by his Aunt). As I write this, our favourite CD is playing: Mahler's *Song of the Earth*. So often Keith and I have listened to it, enraptured: "the music of Heaven", he called it, and so it is.

When Keith first showed signs of dementia, once screaming that I was the Devil and then attacking me with a bread-knife, I panicked. Fortunately we had a competent, understanding doctor, in whom we had been able to confide our homosexuality, and he was generous in giving me advice, as well as treating Keith with pacifying drugs. I have written to him (Dr Evan Klein) to express our deep gratitude for his kind expertise. I know that there are others (individuals or organizations) who would also have helped us in our ordeal of the past four years. Dr Klein put me in touch with a Seniors' Home that offered a program whereby I could deliver Keith into their hands, for most of one day during the week, and, while he was fed and entertained (with games and singing and stories), I was able to do the shopping, washing and other necessary domestic chores of the week, before picking him up in the late afternoon. I am grateful for that as well: I think it saved me from total collapse. Many people have shown us kindness. I am so grateful. May God bless them all.

And Keith showed me such extreme kindness, always, until his illness prevented him. He and I enjoyed so much together, for eight glorious years: classical music (especially Schubert and Mahler), and literature (here we differed in our favourite authors: he admired Thomas Hardy, I adored Jane Austen – many were our fervent debates, after reading passages to each other!), concerts, films, theater, travelling abroad (we toured England and Europe, and went on a Caribbean cruise).

After he began his descent, our times of greatest happiness, and of the deepest and most consoling intimacy (certainly for me, but I think also for Keith), were when I read to him from the Bible (especially Psalm 23), or when we listened together (sometimes in the darkness) to the *Song of the Earth*. The final part of that great composition, "Der Abschied – The Farewell", moved and consoled us more than I could ever describe – not only the music, but the words, in their celebration of noble Comradeship: "I yearn, my Friend, to enjoy the beauty of the evening beside you. Where are you? You have left me alone so long! ... I am seeking peace for my lonely heart..." In my imagination I was the Narrator, awaiting the arrival of the mysterious horseman (who was always Keith in my imagination): "I am waiting for my Friend; I wait to bid him a final farewell."

And that farewell is almost here. The music is enfolding us both (as I write these words) in its ecstatic warmth. When "Der Abschied" ends, repeating and repeating and repeating the one word, "Ewig" – "Eternity, Eternity, Eternity" – Fischer-Dieskau's voice so heart-stoppingly strong and beautiful – as the music fades and fades into silence. And then it will be time for the two of us to follow the silence into our Eternity.

I think that Keith, the horseman, may have reached Eternity already. He is not breathing. His heart is still. I have covered his face. "Eternity, Eternity, Eternity." Silence. Now I will read our Funeral Service; with, for the last time, Psalm 23; then I will pray for God's forgiveness; and finally, just before I drink my final glass of wine, and swallow the pills, I will recite the Blessing that Keith taught me, and that we both love: "May the Lord bless us and keep us, may the light of His countenance shine upon us, and give us His peace. Amen."

I am ready to go.

Please do not ask yourselves if anyone could have "done more" for us. And do not feel that "society" failed us and is somehow responsible for our death. (Once I conversed briefly with a street-person who had rejected all attempts to settle him indoors: "I can only be myself in the open", he told me. And I know I can only be myself with Keith.) As I said, we have received great kindness. Of course "more could have been done" for us, and by us – but that would always be so.

If Keith had remained healthy in mind and body, and I had not contracted ALS (Dr Klein told me four days ago that the tests had confirmed his fears), the decision to depart now would not have become necessary. "Crass Casualty", Keith would have called the facts of our situation, smilingly (one of his favourite Hardy quotations): just very bad luck! (My feet are numb; I have stumbled and fallen several times; climbing the stairs is already difficult, and even holding this ballpoint is a struggle – as you can see from my writing. How long could I go on looking after Keith?)

God's will be done. God bless you all. May He give you peace.

It is time now. Farewell.

(signed) Arnold Holloway

Nos Morituri Te Salutamus

Dear John,

You win! You are a bloody determined bugger, my boy. You would not leave me alone (all those letters & telephone conversations, & four visits in three years), & now *I* won't leave me alone! But I'm an old man, for Christ's sake: seventy-four at last count. Why can't I be left in peace now? Why do I have to do guilt & suffering & shame again, after so many years, so many tears: didn't I do it then? When I was twenty-four and he was

No. I will not do it, John. You took advantage of me, you took me by surprise, with your wide blue eyes fixed on me, that unexpected first meeting. The very picture of innocence – but I know better now, my boy. "Sir, I have been longing to meet you. It is a very great honour, Sir." General Masterman, double War Hero now in his dotage. Met, quite by chance of course, in his local, drinking alone at the bar, again. But I was captured, of course. Captivated, I mean. Vanity, thy name is Vanity. Also I was lonely, still am lonely – lonelier than ever. Also the Canadian accent always attracts my attention, reminding me of a very close friend in the Second War. Brent. So I bought you a pint of bitter & we talked. And talked.

Such a coincidence! Such charming youthful hesitance! "Sir, the barman said you – General Sir David Masterman? – Weren't you at El Alamein & Normandy – ? And a hero of the Great War. Do you – I wonder if you remember my Great-uncle, Sir? Jonathon King, he – I was re-reading his letters from the Western Front recently, & I'm sure he mentioned – No, it was in one of the last letters he wrote his Mother (my Great-grandmother), from Italy, not long before he was killed – my Grandmother gave them to my Father –" Something like that – & much more of the soft-soap. "Sir, I have been longing to meet you. It is a very great honour, Sir." My VC, my being with Montgomery in pursuit of Rommel, et cetera, et cetera. (I could tell you a few things about my relationship with Monty; but I won't.) Oh, you did it well, John, my boy. I admired your acting, & I admire your cunning still. But let me tell you now (since I want to try the impossible, to be totally honest), I suspected, I guessed, I knew, what you were up to, & I could have (should have?) ended our conversation then & there. That would have been easy: I have ended a great many conversations in my life. You might say I am well-practised in the arts of dominance, evasion & concealment.

But, as I say, vanity – & loneliness. They take an ever-increasing toll on one's pride & self-control. Be warned! Also (as you well know – I have told you so), you are a very handsome, personable, witty young man. I liked you from the beginning, & have always enjoyed being with you, & all our dueling discussions, our long conversations; & I will now confess that, when we met, even before you named him, you immediately reminded me, intensely, intolerably, of

This letter too – if I finish it, & decide to post it (which I may not), will further diminish my pride & self-control. But does that matter much now? At my age – & I am a sick man (my doctor tells me that unless I stop drinking, another heart-attack is imminent, the one that will finally do for me) – And here I sit, drinking! Drinking whiskey, on my own (sure mark of the alcoholic!). However, remember, John, your solemn promise at the end of your last visit, my boy, when (clever move if you had psyched me out by then with your "gaydar" – I know how perceptive you are!) you brought your lover Iain with you – Your promise to me, for whatever cunning reason, that anything I told you or tell you is not to be communicated by you to *anyone, will not be*, unless I give explicit permission. You *promised* that, John, & I hold you to that promise. Remember: "On my honour, Sir." This letter is a private, personal communication, to answer your questions, to tell you the truth, the whole truth, insofar as I am able, & while I can. When you have read it, I would prefer that it be burnt; but of course I know that only your conscience will decide what you do with this document. As I said, I am already into the whiskey, so to-night may end as so many of my nights do now, with General Masterman staggering to bed & mercifully falling asleep. Or I may not wake up to-morrow morning. That would be preferable.

You must have noted the date of this letter. Yes, it is the fiftieth anniversary of your great-uncle Jonathon's death. (It is also the date of Shakespeare's birth & Wilfred Owen's death – & it is St George's Day too, forsooth! A good day to die on, if to die is your destiny. I wonder if he thought of that?) In a few months it will be the fiftieth anniversary of the whole Catastrophe of Civilization – of that War which some (including you!) still like to call Great. (That has always been one of my reservations about you, my boy.) Great? Great slaughter, great destruction, oh yes! Great sadness, great stupidity. Great disaster! And we should all feel great compassion for all those cut off so young – I don't read the historians & biographers now, I close my ears to the priests & politicians (though if I'm still here on November 11th, I will no doubt stagger along the streets of London with my fellow-survivors & stand at the Cenotaph & hear the Last Post & try to remember all my dead friends & comrades. Habit or compulsion?) No, I read the Poets now, John; *only* the Poets, especially Wilfred Owen – "the Pity of War, the Pity War distilled" – poems by men who told the truth & were dead before our So Very Great War ended. Dead as your Great-uncle, as my Jonathon, was. – Your Jonathon, my Jonathon. Jonathon. Whom I will not, cannot, forget.

Now I will tell you something, John, that fills me with sorrow & guilt. I do not think you have suspected it, even when commenting on his letters to his mother, the ones you photocopied & sent me. "They are so well-written," you said. "I guess English schoolboys were all so well-educated in those days, especially the Officers because they had been at English public schools." Yes, John, oh yes. I was of course at one of those public-schoolboys, John; as was Jonathon. In fact, that's where he & I first met & – got to know each other. I never mentioned it to you, but I thought you would fasten onto that fact yourself & ask questions about it. Yet, if you noticed it at all (that we were at the same small public school in East Anglia), you clearly did not think that very significant. But it was, oh yes it was. I was three years older than Jonathon; I was a Prefect & Head of House in the year we met. And Jonathon was in my House – in fact, he was my

Fag (I won't waste time & space explaining the implications of that to you – you may anyway be aware of the public-school Prefectorial system, et cetera, through films like *If*). He & I – We fell

What I am in danger of forgetting to tell you is that Jonathon & I, though years & Forms apart, were taught by the same English Master, who of course encouraged all his boys to write poems. (He also encouraged other things, but that is a different story, perhaps: he was a Pedophile.) My poems were poor stuff, as I well recognised (I had no talent in that direction, though I sometimes got high marks for essays). Jonathon, on the other hand, was a good poet, a natural poet; even I could see that. Oh, more than that: a superlative poet. When, during the Second War, I first read Owen's poems, I was stunned: & understood that Jonathon's poems, as I remembered them, were at least their equal in aesthetic power & memorable truth. You are now wondering "Did he write many War Poems? What happened to them?" Yes, he did, John – quite a few – at least two dozen. I read them all; then I destroyed them. Alas, alas. But it was not a wanton act of envy or rejection, John: *it was not*. Jonathon made me promise to burn them if – if he was killed. However, perhaps, I

Should I continue? I am circling the dark centre of my anguish. I don't feel equal to this, John, my boy, my boy – But I know that if I don't write it now (even though I am already tipsy, & also weary, so weary), I will never write it. But I will have to try to be brief.

Jonathon & I fell in love. Such a simple statement, such a bewilderingly intense emotion. Well, we know very well now that it happens, when boys are herded together in adolescence, away from girls; we even admit now that it always did happen, always would happen. Perhaps most boys "grow out of that" & into an orthodox heterosexual future – which was a common expectation of the time. But neither of us did. I married during the Thirties; my wife & I both knew it was a marriage of convenience (she left me ultimately – that is definitely "another story"). Let me also confess (truth, truth!) that I had a long series of discreet liaisons – mainly, during the two Wars, with fellow Officers – only one of which gave me more than temporary satisfaction & relief; & I was careful not to allow myself to love any of them – except Brent – (more of him later, perhaps). (I wonder, John, if you & your Iain are still "partners"? – permit me to doubt it: he seemed less committed than you – but I may be wrong – I hope so. The pain of losing someone you love is insupportable.)

Jonathon & I. Oh, my beloved. My Jonathon, my Jonathon. "Passing the love of women." Well, it certainly surpassed my love for Margaret or hers for me. But then

Then the War came. I was twenty-one, just about to begin my third year at Christ Church, & Jonathon, after brilliant academic achievement at School, especially in the Sixth Form (he enjoyed sport, but wasn't much good at it; I was the Sportsman – Victor Ludorum, Captain of Cricket, Head of School, et cetera) – Jonathon had won a Scholarship to Balliol, he was soon to come up, we would be at Oxford together! Earlier that summer, he had been at my 21st Birthday Party, staying (before & after) at our country house in Devon for three delirious weeks. (Overtones of *Brideshead Revisited*?) My parents approved of him, admired him: "Such a nice boy, such a fine friend" – not knowing, of course, that we were lovers; that we were at that time renewing & strengthening our schoolboy relationship, discovering a passionate intensity that made any separation unimaginable.

Then the anguish began. We both rushed to volunteer, of course. One did, then. One's love of School & Country ordained it. I was immediately sent off for training (I had been a keen member of the OTC at School, of course), was commissioned in the Devonshires, & sent into the trenches in good time for the Somme – which I not only survived but emerged from with a Military Cross, an acknowledged Hero! You know all about that. What you do not know is the suffering Jonathon endured, until 1917. Yes, suffering. it may seem ironic & even paradoxical, that he suffered because (as he bitterly put it) "They think I'm too young to take on the Bosch, so they won't commission me, they just keep me hanging around". His depression was deepened by a bout of quite-severe illness (probably the main reason his commission was delayed), &, I'm sad to say, by my MC: though he came to Buckingham Palace with me & Mother (Father died in 1915) for the Investiture by the King.

The MC business was much exacerbated by the fact that he belonged to a prominent military family (of course you know all about that, they're your ancestors), while my Father had made his money in business. The accursed English class system – I often preached to you on that topic, John, didn't I? I met his Father twice before the War, at Speech Days (he gave the Speech at the second one, in 1911, my last – "Nos Morituri Te Salutamus" – no, that's your joke, isn't it? – it was "Dulce Et Decorum Est" of course, & all that thundering jingoism of the period) – he was then a Colonel, handsome, aloof & intimidating – I felt sorry for Jonathon as the son & heir of such a man – even sorrier, & very embarrassed, when he used me & my sporting prowess to sneer at his own son. I was invited to dinner at the poshest hotel in the town, where the Colonel condescended to his silent wife & son & daughter, & talked only to me, man to man, all through the dinner. I'm sorry – indeed, ashamed – to say I was pleased by the gross flattery of his attentions, his military advice & inside information, his stories of the Boer War – Blood River, Mafeking, et cetera. Probably I played up to him. Yes, I did.

Poor Jonathon. He wanted military achievement so badly, & struggled so hard to purge any jealousy or resentment, especially after my success at the Somme, my MC. During that period, we met only briefly, when I was on leave; & gradually we lost touch, became more & more distant from each other. But then it had become increasingly difficult even to remember one's earlier, civilian life & relationships, while the bombs were exploding in No Man's Land, & snipers were picking off every new Officer who put his head above the parapet – in fact, I wasn't alone in not wanting to think or talk about the Home Front. The trenches became our real home: the Poets were emphatic about that – Wilfred Owen was, & Jonathon was, too, after he had been in the trenches for a year. He had suddenly written, early in 1917, to say that he had been commissioned at last, was going out with his Regiment to France, & when could we meet? I was delighted by the note of excited pleasure in his letter; but we did not meet until the summer of 1918, very near the end of the War.

Of course we both tried to meet earlier, but

Well, I have got through the preliminaries all right, more or less – I hope. Perhaps I'm not as tipsy as I thought (all alcoholics hold their liquor deceptively well), & perhaps I was merely looking for an excuse, to delay what's coming, what must come – Certainly I am not as drunk as I shall become after I finish this letter, my boy, when I set seriously about the next bottle of whiskey. So that I can sleep to-night. I said I'd be honest, John. Now you know this truth at least – you know about the pathetic alcoholic who was once a Soldier worthy of respect, who was even once a Hero – or considered such – Now – Well, I think more & more about the loaded service-revolver in my drawer. Perhaps one of these nights

So we came, Jonathon & I, to Asiago. It is1918: the Very Great War is limping to its dreary end. The German Army is retreating after its last desperate advance, the Americans are rampaging around Europe to "save" us, their exhausted Allies. One of the irritating side-shows that need tidying away is the Austro-Hungarian attempt to escape their noose & humiliate the Italians. It seems an especially nasty trick of Fate to have brought Jonathon & me together there & then. (You have had my variant of *Brideshead Revisited*; now prepare yourself for my *Journey's End*.)

I was there first – just as I preceded Jonathon into the War itself. It was a shock to see his name in the dispatch – & there was to be another shock soon after his arrival. We had not seen each other, not even been in communication with each other, for over a year. So seeing him again was almost like meeting a stranger. I guess he felt the same. We had both changed – *been* changed – more than we could know. The moment I saw him I knew he was finished – bone-weary, shell-shocked (now, as you know, it's called Post-Traumatic Stress Disorder) – he was so clearly at the end of his endurance. And something else I saw in his face: embarrassment, shame. While the Sergeant watched & listened, I tried ineffectually to reach him across the barriers of Army discipline & our near-estrangement ("Stand at ease! Captain Lord, welcome to your new Regiment. Glad to have you! We are very short-handed. Two officers wounded & sent Home recently. From the frying-pan into the fire, eh! Your situation, I mean. We are expecting orders to attack very soon." Et cetera. And finally, "I would be glad if you could meet me in my tent this evening at nine for a detailed briefing about your responsibilities.") We did meet. We did.

John, I do not want to see you again. Please do not take that personally. If you came unannounced again, as at our first meeting, I would turn my back on you & refuse to talk to you. Can you begin to understand why? You will. And the anguish – I guess I am not brave enough to endure any more. Thinking about Jonathon, being forced to re-live our last moments together – Intolerable. You may not know how very much you resemble him, John. Not only family resemblance – though you are very like him, in appearance & personality – your Canadian qualities seem even to strengthen the resemblance. Let me also confess that I

How can I say this? Please do not be offended. It is this: You have become a major force in an old man's life. During periods between our meetings, between your letters, I have thought obsessively about you, dreamt about you, & sometimes I guess I even talk & write like a Canadian ("I guess", for Christ's sake!). John, let me be direct: I am in love with you. Or is it Jonathon within you whom I love? And I cannot bear that any longer, I cannot endure that. I cannot look into your eyes, again, my boy, my boy! Do you know (laugh at this!) I actually found myself obsessively jealous of that pretty boyfriend you sprang on me – your Iain. Up to then, I wasn't even sure that you are homosexual – homosexual like Jonathon, like me, like Wilfred Owen. We talked always about War, both Wars, you & I – rarely talked about ourselves or each other – but I should have guessed – I even dreamt of you having sex with Iain, & longed to be him. A seventy-four- year-old man! Tormenting himself. Behaving like a lovelorn teenager. Behaving as I did with Jonathon all those years ago, when we were schoolboys – & for that brief time afterwards, before the War broke into all our lives.

Let me finish this. I must finish this.

I am filled with anger, John, in addition to all the other churning emotions. That Jonathon was treated as a criminal rather than the brave soldier & loving man he was, & is (for he is alive for me, & will always be alive in you). That his own Father could – (Do you know Owen's "Parable of the Old Man & the Young"? Read it, then re-read it.) To see him standing there – Jonathon, my Jonathon – broken, exhausted, despised by his own Father – & worse, as I found soon afterwards, when the next dispatch arrived &

Yes, anger. Why wasn't I angry long ago? Why – Only now, now, in this drunken rage, have I decided that I will not participate in this year's celebrations on November 11th. Remembrance Day! I will not – Assuming that I am still alive then, I will not desecrate the memory of Jonathon again. Ever again. I will not. *I will not.*

Now let me finish this. The day after Jonathon joined my regiment, a dispatch, together with a personal letter, arrived from his Father, your famous & eminent Great-grandfather, General Sir Arthur King, stationed then in Paris, I think. Helping to run our Oh So Very Great War into the ground. His instructions to me were very clear. I was directed to organise & oversee a tribunal to try Jonathon for a heinous crime. He had been accused by a fellow-Officer of conducting a sexual relationship with his Batman. Buggery. There was "inescapable evidence", including the confession of the Batman & the testimony of a second fellow-Officer, who claimed to have come across two men "consorting together". The outcome was inescapable: a court-martial was necessary, for the sake of maintaining Discipline. In the accompanying letter, General King expressed his horror, not only at the "shockingly reprehensible behaviour" of his son, but also at the fact that the sexual relations were with a servant, a member of the lower classes. As I have said, I had had homosexual relations, but only with fellow Officers – & I am ashamed to say that I was shocked too by Jonathon's having sex with a servant (the iniquitous class-system again!) – I too thought (God forgive me) that Jonathon's behaviour was "utterly repugnant", "unforgivable", & if publicised would certainly bring disgrace on his Family, his Regiment, our School. There was only one way out of "this damnable mess". Yes, I knew what would come next. Phrased so delicately. "I trust you, David. I admire your bravery & integrity. You are a man of Honour. You are the Son I would wish to have had. You are Jonathon's friend, & will feel as I do that his name & reputation should be protected. He will listen to you. I know he will."

What did he want me to do? Oh, I knew. I knew. And, no doubt, somewhere whispering at the back of my mind was the thought that General King could advance my military career, recommend me for medals & promotion – & he did. All I had to do was

I do not wish to recall our final meeting in any detail. I sent for Jonathon. I told him about the accusation & the necessity for a court-martial, "however much I might wish that –" Standing at attention, gazing at me, he simply nodded. He knew. "To protect your name & reputation, & your Family's, & the School's –" He nodded. Then he stepped forward, looked deeply into my eyes, took my hand & raised it to his lips. "Goodbye," he whispered. "I love you." He stepped back, saluted, turned, & went. I saw him once more, briefly, after the order came next morning – the enemy were attacking, our regiment was to advance, was to counter-attack. As he moved forward, leading the men he had only recently met, he turned his head towards me, & he smiled, & winked.

Supporting the Italians, we defeated the Austrians, in a bitter battle. There were too many casualties. I was slightly wounded myself, leading a final attack on the Austrian positions – the attack that was said to have turned the tide in our favour. His Company were falling back in disarray, I had to rally them & lead them forward. Afterwards, with my arm bandaged, I watched our dead & wounded being carried to the field-station on stretchers. One of the dead was Jonathon. He had been shot once, through the heart. I could not bear to look at his corpse for more than a moment.

There. You have it. Is it what you want? Is it what you suspected? Is it what you want?

Jonathon's Father, your Great-grandfather, General King, sent a dispatch congratulating our Regiment on a "brilliantly courageous performance". He also sent a personal note to me, lamenting the death of his son. "His Mother & I will always miss him, but we are proud that he gave his life for his King & Country." I replied very briefly, saying only that Jonathon had died bravely in the heat of the battle. As I know he did. I never heard from General King again – but before the end of our Very Great War I was promoted to Colonel, & awarded a VC for my "extreme courage & superb leadership in desperate circumstances," et cetera. And now

Duty. Now I have done my duty. That has nothing to do with Honour, John. Indeed, it seems to have little to do with – It is my final – perhaps my only – tribute to the man I loved & betrayed. I have loved only two other men, I think: my Canadian adjutant in the Second War, & you. Brent was killed driving me in a jeep in the Western Desert. Look out, my boy! The bullet that killed him was meant for me. Those who have got closest to me have always lost their lives, while David Masterman lives on & on, in pain & shame. But now, at last, it is time for him to go. I *will* send you this letter, my dear John, my dearest Jonathon. Do with it what you will. Farewell.

Yours sincerely,
David

Are You Still There?

–Chris? This a good time for a chat?

–12:30 a.m.? – *No*. No. But, hey, why not? I had too many damn coffees at that party, what happens when you've had too many damn beers and you know you shouldn't try to drive home like that but you do – and now I won't be able to sleep for hours. So – all right, fire away.

–Yeah, that was quite the party! I had too much to drink too. Why does one celebrate turning forty? I won't, that's for sure. Old age ain't for me.

–Me neither – and I'm thirty-nine, as you may remember, so my fortieth's pretty damn near! It's not a celebration – more like a wake, I think. Jim kindly reminded me I was next in line for execution, when I got through the crowd and close enough to talk to him. So many guys there I hadn't seen forever! And some I didn't know.

–23rd of November. Sagittarius, just missed Scorpio. You're five years older than me. Of course I remember. You were twenty-eight, weren't you, when I met you?

–At that damn wedding reception. Your brother marrying my cousin. And now they're divorced, and my cousin's into her third marriage – looks as if we didn't do a good job, eh? No wonder all those happy heteros out there didn't want us homos getting into the act, they were protecting us from the institution of marriage, they just had our fucking good in mind. I remember I was bored as hell, sitting there, when I noticed you giving me the eye.

–*You* giving *me* the eye, you mean! I was just coming out then, I was a baby of twenty-three, didn't even know if I was gay – how could I know enough to give you the eye?

–Well, you did. Must have come naturally. I can see you now, all fresh and youthful, real eye-candy! And then you got up and walked to the john, and I followed you, and the rest is history – mainly bad history, eh? You were always the active one, never wanted to settle down. Knew I loved you, I told you often enough, gave you everything I had, everything I could afford, and yet – Ah no, I'm not getting into this. No. It's the damn beer talking. After all that fucking coffee, and all that pissing, you'd think the beer – So, are you still so active, still into the bars and bathhouses scene?

–Not so much. But you know I always went for guys my age, or older, and that's where you find them. Not at parties or the gym. And the guys on the internet are mostly liars and cheats and one-night stands. But I always tell them I'll only go so far, which means mutual masturbation, maybe a bit of oral, definitely no anal. Jerking-off, especially with another guy, that gives me what I need now. Why risk AIDS? And they're saying – someone told me this tonight – they're saying now that even oral's not safe the way we used to think.

–Well, I'm not into that damn wild stuff either, now. I had all of that, did enough of it to get damn near to the fucking edge. That's when you look over and say Whoa, eh? – enough's enough. Got myself tested couple of months ago, HIV-negative. Big fucking sigh of relief. Like you say, why risk getting AIDS? Not worth the squirt.

–So looks like we came out at the same place, more or less.

–Yeah, but you're younger, you should be still out there, having a good time. You got a damn good body, better than mine – those pecs, that big fat cock, I remember it well! – and I guess you work out two or three times a week?

–You're not so bad yourself, Chris, whatever you say. You never valued your body, never valued yourself. That first time with you – the first weeks, before we started living together – I was out of my mind with pleasure, I was ecstatic, couldn't wait for the next fuck, I thought you were by far the best a man could ever be, in bed, out of bed, in every way I could think of. You were Mister Perfection.

–And then what happened? I agree, we were a damn fine team then, good friends and good fuck-buddies. I'll tell you what happened. Your mother, your father, your brothers, that's what happened. Decided I was snatching you from the cradle. You said Must be open, can't live a lie, persuaded me to meet them. Fucking mistake, I knew that at the time, but you wouldn't listen to me. I remember your father, propelled from behind, of course, by your mother – I came to loathe that woman, even more than you know – my turn to be open and honest, eh? – He summoned me into his impressive bigshot-lawyer's office on Bay Street, and gave me a fucking lecture about how I was interfering in your education, you had been getting on so well at U of T with your research for the doctorate, and now I was distracting you, endangering your whole fucking future, I was just a fucking damn nuisance, a major bloody menace to your family's happiness and good fortune. And when that didn't work, your mother set your two older brothers onto me, the jock one, Bernie, and the other jock one, Norman, was that his name? They ambushed me in a bar, must have followed me there, and took turns threatening me, hissing into my ears from both sides. Why did you – ?

–I know you blame me for all that, Chris. But I didn't even know it was happening. When you told me a bit about that, I did try, very hard, truly, I did try to stop it happening. My mistake – well, it was *our* mistake, remember how we talked about it, and we both agreed, or I thought we did, to be open and honest? First off, I confided to my mother, a few months after we met, when I was about to move in with you. I thought she could be trusted, that she would even support us – she and I'd always been close. But no, she went ballistic. Not as if she didn't have two other sons, even already had two grandchildren. Actually, I think it was mainly the Catholic thing, she genuinely believed I was on my way to Hell.

–Homophobia, it was sheer damn fucking homophobia, we should have kept our relationship secret. It was nobody else's business. She was a snob too. It wasn't just that I wasn't female, it was that I was an uneducated slob in her eyes. I don't think I ever told you how she invited me to meet her for a coffee downtown, and at first she was all sweet understanding, how was my job going, she wished she had my ability in home decoration, etcetera, etcetera – and then suddenly she was sobbing and attacking me. Oh, her lovely boy, so handsome and charming and innocent, she'd always known you needed to be protected from older men like me, who would want to lead you into sin, ruin your life – I wanted to tell her to fuck off, but of course I didn't. And all the time you just let it happen.

–What could I do, Chris? Cut myself off from my family? And – maybe you've forgotten – your friends didn't help. They made it very clear that they didn't like me, I was too, what, serious and upper-class and *educated* – I enjoyed political arguments, but they didn't want that, and I knew almost nothing about hockey, the Great Canadian Game, which as you know I never played, because I had weak ankles and the doctor advised against, and to them that was a disgrace in itself – and also I didn't find any pleasure in sitting all night drinking myself blind drunk with them, listening to them yelling their homophobic jokes. I never understood how you could stand that – you didn't go all the way with them, I know that, and they even knew, some of them, that you were gay, and teased you about it, yet you were part of the gang, and I wasn't and never could be. Like my family trying to get rid of you, your friends tried to get rid of *me*. That's when I joined a gym and started to work out every day, so at least I got that out of it – guess I wanted to impress them, and especially impress you. But nothing I did made a difference – or enough of a difference.

–Why are we talking about all those damn problems of the past? It's just because we're both drunk, and tired too. We shouldn't have started this – I should have refused to get into this conversation with you. Won't do any good for either of us. Dirty water under the bridge. We've both moved on, haven't we?

–I guess it's because I saw you tonight, across the room, just like when I first saw you. That's why I called you, first time in years, quite a few years. And I wanted to talk to you at the party, but I couldn't. It would have been hard enough just to get close to you, with all your friends around you, and yelling so loud we wouldn't have heard each other anyways. But when I got back to my apartment, and looked around me, and thought about my life, and how I don't have anyone to share it with – I've tried, Chris, I've had a few lovers along the way, but the ones who didn't want just a quick fuck, they were mostly married men cheating on their wives, enduring unhappy marriages, and they longed for a relationship with me, with any man, but how could that work out? It was impossible – it wore me down, I guess I got tired of all the angst. Does it have to be like that? I ask myself that over and over. And I think of you. Do you ever think of me?

–Fuck off, I don't want any of this. Know what I think? We should have fucking talked about all that stuff when it mattered – when it *could* matter, when we were still together, before you walked out on me. You did do that, remember? *You* walked, not me. Found someone better, who *really* loved you. So don't give me all this fucking bloody sob-stuff now. *Don't!* I'm going to end this damn conversation right now. It's too late.

–No, Chris. Just give me a few more minutes. I know we both got to get some sleep. But I couldn't sleep anyway now, if we don't finish this. Please. Listen, I made a mistake, I made lots of mistakes. I didn't know that what we had was so good, I guess I was always hoping for better, looking for better. I was immature, Chris. I paid too much attention to my family, I took your friends too seriously. I should have concentrated on what matters – that we were happy together – I was *so* happy, it was so *good* with you, it's like we were made for each other – Are you still there?

–Yeah. I guess I'm still here. But –

–And I noticed you were on your own tonight? And one of your friends said – yes, I asked him about you, Chris – he said you and your partner had split up. So I thought maybe we could -

–Oh, Danny. Oh, Danny. Mark had to fly over to Boston, his mother is dying. He hasn't left me, he called me before the party, he's with his family. Danny? Are you still there?

–Chris. I'm sorry. I feel – I feel humiliated. Why did I call you? What a fool I am. I apologize. I'm sorry. I'm sorry. So now let's get to bed and try to sleep, eh?

–Danny. Look, we had good times together. It was good, very good, while it lasted. But nothing lasts for ever, that's just the way it is, that's life. Everything changes, we got to enjoy the good times between, got to remember those, and enjoy them. – But one more thing. I lied.

–Lied?

–When I told you I had the HIV test. I said the result was negative. It wasn't. It was positive, Danny. I haven't told Mark yet, I don't know what he'll do.

–Oh. I'm sorry, Chris. I'm so very sorry. I don't know what to say. If there's anything I can do –

–Nothing. Say nothing. And now I got to go, Danny. I'm so fucking tired I'll fall on my face if I don't get to bed. So – goodbye, Danny. Sleep well, my friend.

–Goodbye, Chris. If only – No. Nothing. Sleep well, my friend.

Fairy Frolicsome's Family

After Barry left him, Tom collapsed into a deep depression. Withdrawn, suicidal. They'd been together for over six years – how *could* he just walk out like that? As if falling for a pretty boy half his age could cancel all the love, all the promises, all the joyful experiences ...

Then Martin banged into Tom's life, noisy cheerful Martin whose condo was in the same building and who had smiled and chatted whenever they met in the elevator. One night, three weeks after Barry's departure, he knocked at Tom's door – loudly, insistently. Reluctant and irritated, Tom unlocked and opened it. Martin proffered a bottle of wine – "Guaranteed to cure all ills, when shared with a good-looking and thirsty neighbour."

They drank, they talked. And Martin stayed the night: both of them were starved for sex, and here it was, easy and satisfying. But their conversation before that, while they worked their way through the bottle's contents, and then through another bottle's contents, brought profound and lasting change into their lives.

As always, Martin was direct: "I heard Barry left you. Bastard!"

And Tom was evasive: "Well. He ..."

"What? He what? I heard he ran off with some twinkie."

"Well ... They're in Vancouver. He wrote me from there a few weeks ago – that he'd fallen in love, totally in love, with ... Whatsisname. He said it was the biggest thing he'd ever ..."

"Tom, I never felt Barry deserved you. Know that? Don't make excuses for him. And you're so faithful – as well as being a knockout. I mean that. Ever since I moved in here – nine months must be now – I've been making eyes at you, didn't you notice? But *you* only had eyes for *him*. While he was ... Well, you must know he got around."

"We had an open relationship, Martin."

"Right. I've had one or two of those too. But no more, no more, no more. Next time it's for good, it's marriage. Is it too soon for me to propose? Of course I'm assuming you are attracted to me, now I've made you notice me – my perfect body, my intelligence, my loud voice, my sense of humour, my capacity for true and loyal love ..."

A week later, friends and acquaintances learned that Martin and Tom were an Item, and, two weeks after that, a party in Martin's condo celebrated the fact. Tom's friends were glad to see him again happy, optimistic. And Martin introduced Tom to his mother, a gaunt vivacious woman who was approving – she'd been oh so impressed by Tom, from the moment Martin first mentioned him; he'd sounded just right, he *was* just right; at last, at last – it really was high time that Martin settled down.

Martin was an only child. His mother was divorced; well-known in Toronto's higher circles for her involvement in a variety of well-publicized charitable endeavours. And, Martin added, "she's a serial adulterer – adulteress. I see more of her in 'City Life' than in the flesh – you know, 'Parties, Culture & Society', especially 'Parties', in the *National Post* – but she does call me for a chat most Sunday evenings. I never see or hear at all from my father" – who was now living, with his second wife and her two children, in Calgary, where he was a big-shot oil-company lawyer. "I'm quite rich too, by the way – my grandaddy made a fortune in real estate – of course that's why Mother can dispense big bundles of bucks to all her charities."

Tom's family? "Oh, my father died about ten years ago, liver cancer, but he never forgave me for being gay – which, as you well know, is an evil state, contrary to God's law, as well as being a slur on my father's manhood and shamefully making me the last of his line – the latter sin especially resented. I would see him on family occasions, like my mother's birthday, or my sister's, or his, and he would eke out a few words, like 'Hullo, I hope you've been keeping well?' while looking over my left shoulder. When he was in hospital, I hoped we could be reconciled, but it was too late, he was too angry at first and too drugged by the end ..."

"But your mother's still alive?"

"Yes. She's my biggest problem, really. Why am I telling you all this boring stuff? All right, it's because she and I were very close when I was a boy; I wasn't much good at sports – to my father's oft-expressed disappointment – so I guess I tried to please Mom – played the piano and painted portraits of flowers and so on. She kept the peace, more or less, between Father and me, but my sister, Vera – she *was* good at sports, in fact she was my opposite in every way, confident where I was shy, smart where I was slow until they realized why – that my hearing was poor and my eyesight weak. My poor father! To cut a long story short, I kept out of his way, and my sister's, and lived my own life – I work in a travel-agency, I think you know that – so I can travel often, and I do, in Europe especially. But my mother – it was all right between us before my father died, we would meet for meals in restaurants, and go to the occasional movie or concert together. But then, can you believe it, on his deathbed he made her swear never to have anything more to do with me until I 'came to my senses.'"

"And she – ?"

"In her generation, a married woman obeyed her husband, he was lord and master – and my father prided himself on being alpha-male. He must have bullied her into doing it – well, of course he did, she was crying when she told me, after the funeral, what she'd promised, and … So that's how it is … But I persuaded my sister to always call me if there was anything to report. She's married, lives in Texas, four children, but she calls my mother every few nights. So at least I know she's all right, physically and financially. Dad left the house to her, and most of his money to her and my sister. But weren't we going to discuss – ?"

"Living arrangements. Yes, I think you're right, what you suggested, Tom. I'll move in with you and rent out my condo. Jim, you know him, he has a rich French friend visiting soon who wants a summer let in the Village, for Pride etcetera. And then we'll see about selling it. And we'll get married next Spring, tra-la, and then all our possessions will be jointly owned, and we'll be happy together ever after. How's that for a plan?"

The call from Tom's sister came a few days later. "Tom, Mummy's had a fall. She's in hospital. I can't come at the moment. I got through to her and told her she would have to stop the nonsense about not connecting with you. Bloody childish behaviour, anyway – you know I've always thought that. She never should have let herself be pushed around by Dad. So please, Tom, would you – ? I should also say she's been sounding a bit confused lately, I mean even before her fall, when I called her – I didn't say anything to you because ... So will you visit her and call me to say what you think, how serious it is? I'll come as soon as I can. The neighbours on both sides have keys, you know that, so if she needs anything from the house you can get it for her."

Tom came back perturbed and upset after his first hospital visit. "She didn't know me. Thought I was her brother, told me to stop riding her bicycle. The brother was killed in an accident when he was a boy, riding his bike, she once told me that. Then a nurse took me aside and asked what my plans were, for when she'd be ready to leave – said that would likely be soon, and they're short of beds and so on – was Mum on waiting-lists of homes for seniors? What should I do?"

"Oh, Tom, that's a no-brainer. We bring her here."

"Here? How can we – ?"

"To live with us. We can make arrangements, I'll look after her in the mornings – I can do my stuff on E-mail from here, the Minister won't mind, just so long as he's well-briefed for Question Period and gets his Speeches – and you can do the afternoons – or we can get a part-time nurse – Or perhaps we could move in with her, into your family's house I mean – elderly people do better in their own home, surrounded by their own things – you could work it out with your sister, couldn't you?"

"But you haven't even met my mother."

"That's why I'm coming with you when you visit her tomorrow."

They found Tom's mother sitting in a wheel-chair beside her bed. She was dozing.

"Hullo, Mum. It's Tom."

Her eyes opened briefly, then flickered, and closed.

Martin kissed her on the forehead. "Wake up, Mrs Wingate" he said loudly. "My name is Fairy Frolicsome. What do you think of that? I'm the fabulous Fairy Frolicsome!" and he capered round the room, flapping his arms and hands like wings.

She opened her eyes, frowned, and pursed her lips. "You can't be a fairy. You're a man."

"Oh, men can be fairies, ma'am. All the best men are fairies. We've come to fly away with you!" He moved behind the wheel-chair and pushed it towards the door.

She frowned again, glancing at Tom. "Who's *he*?"

"Oh, he's Fairy Fuddle-duddle, a.k.a. Fairy Fart-britches – But I call him Fairy Fun-to-be-with." Martin turned and winked at Tom, who was smiling in embarrassment.

They pushed Tom's mother slowly round the ward. Nurses greeted her, smiled at them. When they were back in her room, "Can I be a fairy too?" she asked.

"You *are* a fairy, my dear. You're Fairy Flora."

"Fora?"

"Flora. Because you're pretty as a flower." He bent to kiss her again.

She glared at Tom. "It's *my* bike, you know it is, I never gave you per ... perfusion ... to ride it. Daddy gave it to *me*. For my birthday. You squished yours, you wasted it. So now..." Her eyes closed and her head fell sideways.

Tom went in search of her nurse, and was told at the desk that she was busy with another patient but would be along shortly – it was time for Jessie to be back in bed anyway.

In the car, Tom sat stiff and silent behind the steering-wheel.

"What's the matter?" Martin asked after a few minutes."What's the matter, my dear? Did I upset you? I'm sorry if I said or did ... My big mouth, I didn't mean to –"

"I was thinking, what are we, just empty shells, if our memories are gone."

"Oh no. Not completely. Alzheimer's can't take away everything we are. Your mother is still an individual, she's still Jessie Wingate, she's still your mother, even if she can't recognize you now. You are still there, somewhere inside her mind and feelings."

"And I was thinking about a dream I had last night. Only the very end of it, that's all I ever remember if I dream, which isn't often anyway. So there was my mother, in a blue dress, and she was standing in the garden, which she loved so much – and she turned to me, and smiled, and then she hugged me, and kissed me, and she whispered 'I love you so much. I wish I had always accepted you just as you are, Tom, and I wish I had made your father accept you too. How much time we wasted, how much love we lost.' I can still hear her saying that: '... how much love we lost, how much love we lost.'"

"And she *did* say it. That wasn't a dream, my dear – it *happened*, I know it did."

Tom turned to Martin. "Hold my hand. Thank you. Thank you. And – I was thinking that I love you and I love you and I love you, and that you are the most unselfish man I have ever known."

"Oh no, you're wrong there, my dear. I am the most *selfish* man that ever *lived*. I told you, I have always longed for a family. A real family. Always. Now that I have one, do you think I'll ever let it go?"

A Perfect Arrangement

Jill

I'm not joking. Mummy didn't have to put up with Great Aunt Bertha's demands and tantrums for eleven years. Well, the old Witch *did* ultimately leave me her house, as promised. Five bedrooms – much too big for me, so I'm thinking of selling it and moving on. Where to? That's one troublesome question I have to answer, and *soon*. My life is a mess. Everyone either hates me or pities me. Then Emily's illness and death. And Colin, poor Colin. When Emily died, after dreadful suffering, he and I were thrown together again. Well, *before* she died, when she asked for me, when I'd come to their apartment and he'd open the door and chat while I took off my coat and boots; and then later, in the hospital where, as she slept her drugged sleep, we'd sit on opposite sides of the bed, each holding a hand, and we couldn't help looking at each other. Or *I* couldn't. Colin, oh Colin! You'd smile slightly, that sad smile. But we never spoke to each other then – hardly ever talked at all, in fact, during those long painful weeks. Emily's husband, and Emily's sister. Doing our duty, expressing our love for her in the only way left. Then the funeral. And the reception afterwards. Well, I should have had more self-control. But

Colin

she came across, *wove* across, spilling wine on her parents' pristine all-white carpet, and she had this tipsy grin – as her mother, my mother-in-law, tears still running down her cheeks, is finishing a long gasping speech to me on the extreme pain of losing a daughter – "It's against Nature, Colin, your child dying before you, that's what makes it even worse than *your* loss, dear boy" – and she seized Jill's tilting wine-glass, placed it carefully on the mantelpiece, and caught her by an arm – and Jill slurred "Shorry, Mum" and giggled, "I know I shouldn't be drunk, and I shouldn't be *shmiling* like this, but what the hell, I can't help it" – and her mother slapped her hard on the cheek and hissed "You're making a show of yourself, and at your sister's funeral, have some respect" – and she turns to me, "Colin, won't you please – ? Take her into the kitchen and give her some coffee" – so I take Jill's arm, she leans on me, we moved slowly into the kitchen – where she suddenly pushed me against the fridge and kissed me, a slobbery kiss and "Colin," she says loudly, "I love you, I always loved you, even when you were –" and

Caroline

that's how I found them. Unbelievable! She was clinging to him, arms round his neck, and he was gaping helplessly over her head. I was less shocked by the fact that she was drunk and out of control than by hearing her bellowing "I love you, I love you" in that ridiculous way! Right after Emily's funeral! I mean – Colin had just buried his wife! Emily was her *sister* and Colin was Emily's *brother-in-law*! And also, I have to be honest about this, just when I was thinking that at last, *at last*, she was beginning to understand herself and what she needs, and how much she means to me, how I have always loved *her*! Since high-school – always, always! And she told me, just two weeks ago – we talked, she was so tired, she said, *exhausted*, psychologically as well as physically – she came to my apartment, just *arrived*, at night, and cried like a baby in my arms – "I can't take any more of this, Carrie, I *can't*, I *can't* – going to the hospital every day, straight from the Library, and seeing her suffering like that, *dying*, when she was always so *alive*, Carrie" – and I persuaded her to lie down on my bed for a while and rest, and later I took her a cup of tea after she'd had some sleep. And she sat there, on the side of my bed, and sipped the tea, and she said "What makes it much worse is Col – he's always there, I can't even be alone with my own sister – I know he's her husband, but he never loved her, so why would he pretend to now, when she's dying?" I listened to her, and I longed to hug her tight and kiss her, and tell her how much I loved her, but I knew it wasn't the right time. Also

Hugh

he felt really sorry for her. She would sit on the other side of Emily's bed, in the hospital, and he would be sitting opposite her, both of them holding one of Emily's hands. They would sit in silence for hours, he said, in total silence. Sometimes he was aware of her gazing at him with disturbing intensity, and he said he didn't know what to do about that. He didn't feel it would be right to smile at her, or talk to her – not with Emily dying between them. When Col and I first met, and became lovers, three years ago, he mentioned that he had once been in love with Jill, as schoolboy and schoolgirl, but she was always so *intense* and possessive that she scared him. And then he met her sister, and Emily was seemingly quite different, so casual and undemanding. So he married her – big mistake, but it was sort of on the rebound. "I know you think I had no right to marry a woman, because I knew I was gay," he said, "but I hadn't met you yet, and I wanted children, Hugh – I've always loved children, I wanted to be a father, but –" But there were no children. Emily's health was too poor and "We didn't ever fuck much anyway. She said it hurt, and I was already having sex with men at the baths – that started even before we married, as you know. And then I met you, and you changed my life." We were both married at that time, Col and I, to women I mean, and that gave us common ground, an understanding of boundaries, limitations. Where we differed was that, when I got married, I didn't know I was gay – but somehow my brother-in-law John did, and he soon seduced me. And I discovered that I liked it, that I was gay too. I decided to tell Deirdre, not about John of course, just about me, and she went through the roof – betrayal, betrayal of her, betrayal of my wedding-vows, and so on and so on. Made my life miserable, until I met Col at the baths, and we talked, and worked out a future for ourselves, getting together discreetly two or three times a week. When Deirdre wanted a divorce so she could marry Adam, I agreed immediately. Then, a few months later, Emily fell seriously ill and was hospitalized. Cancer. Col didn't abandon her, just when she needed him most – if he had, he wouldn't have been the man I love. However, we thought that, when inevitably she died, we could finally live together, even get married. Unfortunately Jill had other ideas. She told him that Emily's last words were she wanted him to marry *her*, and she told him that she had always loved him, he must know that, and that he loved her too, it was destiny, but

Albert

I was the one who found out the truth about Colin and Hugh, and Jill and Caroline. Quite by accident, see, but bloody fortunate for all four of them, as it turned out! Trudy always managed the home great, and such an efficient mother too, she didn't need me, didn't *want* me around. So I would go on short golfing holidays, meet the guys in a hotel, "to relax," I'd say, "the doc says I must, so much stress being a CEO these days" – and some of the relaxation, maybe I should be ashamed to say this, was with a couple gorgeous whores in the bar and then my room, after the eighteenth hole – somehow I always liked two, taking turns to give it to me. Then, the night after Emily's funeral, I was in a hotel bar in Burlington when, I couldn't believe my eyes, I see my son-in-law Colin, the Paragon of Virtue I always thought he was, though I wondered sometimes what he did with his dick – see, I knew he wouldn't be getting any from Emily, she was like her mother, didn't enjoy sex, you could see that when any man came near her. And there he is, in a dark corner, hugging and *kissing* another guy! So I order two Rickard's and mosey over – "Hey, you two, thought you might need some lubrication." Colin's expression was worth the price of admission and then some! I kept the game going a bit longer, and the other guy just kept quiet and just looked at me while my son-in-law stuttered and tried to explain how they were old friends and liked to socialize every now and then – "I can see *that,*" I said, and invited them to have dinner with me, in a way that they couldn't refuse. So then I really got to know about them, that they were both homos, in love, Colin and Hugh, and I found that I *liked* Hugh. Honest, direct guy. And I thought how Colin hadn't got it at home, and how he should have married Jill not Emily, except *she* couldn't ever keep a boyfriend. And as I was thinking that, I suddenly knew why. How come I was so blind, even when I saw that Caroline gazing at her? I go to have a pee, and Hugh follows, and stands next to me, and says can I help them? It's Jill, she's trying to persuade Colin to marry her, and he's so damn decent, Hugh says, and his conscience so over-active, that he might just do that. Obvious what *I* had to do! I cornered Jill at the soonest opportunity and told her I knew her secret – "What secret, Dad?" – "Caroline loves you, and you love her." Well, to cut it short, Jill bursts into tears, I call Caroline and ask her to come over, and I leave them to it. Fortunately Trudy was out at one of her church ladies' groups, and by the time she comes home it's all arranged. The double-wedding was spectacular, as I wanted it to be – hey, *I* was paying for it! Two couples ecstatically happy! Trudy wouldn't attend – she said the marriages were immoral, and an insult to Emily's memory. I say if Emily was in a state to pay attention to our human silliness, she would surely have loved it all, like her Daddy did, and wished them well, told them to go for it! And the two couples moved into the big house Jill inherited from that old misery Bertha, the bossiest big sister any guy ever had, the Sister from Hell – she would probably have been just as mad about the whole thing as Trudy is, and it would be just as much her loss, in my opinion. The gals are on the main floor, see, and the guys on the second floor. They get together for most meals, sharing the cooking, as well as all the other housework. When I was young, there were still flower-children who lived in communes – my parents disapproved, of course, but I loved all that – a pity it didn't continue for my generation. Perhaps our children can re-create it? I get invited to dinner often, by Jill and Caroline and Colin and Hugh, and I enjoy, more than I could ever say, the food and the drink and the conversation and the companionship and the friendship and the fun, the fun, the *fun*. It's the happiest household you could ever imagine! If I'm not too drunk on wine and laughter by the end of the meal, I propose a toast – "God bless your Perfect Arrangement, guys. May it last forever!" They laugh. I guess they think I'm joking, but

Going Home

Pay attention, you!

Yes, you, Milton. Of course you can't see me, so don't gape about – you look cretinous when you do that! Never paid any attention to posture, did you, just slouched; and no clothes-sense either, I had to do it all, choose your clothes, buy them, even *dress* you, baby. Why the fuck did I do that? What was the reward – and don't tell me you kept yourself just for me, I know you didn't. You're a *slut*, Milton! Can you hear that? Yes, I see you smiling that crooked smile of yours, I see you glancing around wondering how it is you think you can still hear me. Slut, slut, slut, slut! Why do I care about you at all, especially *now*? But alas, I do. My over-developed sense of duty and responsibility survives? Maybe.

But I love you too, I miss you – if only I could touch you! Milton! All the times I could have and didn't. And now I can't even see you properly, it's – what is that quotation? – "through a glass darkly". Sort of out of focus. And who knows how long that will last – I wonder if you're even fading right now, or I am – we better be quick. Well, *I* better be. I guess you don't know I'm here – I mean, not in the casket, that's only my body, so don't go on gaping at it – that face in there makes me look like a clown, all that make-up, lipstick – no taste, so embarrassing. *Here.* Look here. Wherever that is!

And there *he* is. Terry. What if he hadn't come? But of course he would – he's so fucking responsible, and honest, so *upright.* When he whispered, with tears glinting in his bloodshot eyes, that he would never have another partner, that he loved only me, could never even *imagine* having sex with another man, or living with another man, he meant it big time. Six years later and he still doesn't have another partner! Said he could understand why I was leaving him for a younger man, such a beautiful younger man. You, Milton! A bit of exaggeration there, but I guess that was Terry all over, generous to a fault. Oh I admire you, Terry, you are a truly good man. But alas, I got bored.

So now let's do it.

Pay attention! Well, you can't control anything once you're finally gone, of course. Come to that, I couldn't control that much when I was still a fully-functioning human-being. So I better get a move on. Here comes Terry, up the steps. Signs the book. Looks very Terry in his grey suit, black tie, etcetera – the whole mourning thing. Didn't have to do that, Terrykins! After the shitty way I treated you, baby! Can you hear me? I guess looking up like that suggests you are aware of something in the air.

Now into the chapel. Will he view my corpse? No, just takes a seat near the back, sits there very still. Chapel filling up – well that's a slight exaggeration – but getting quite respectable now. One thing about the gay community, they love a funeral, free show with lots of emotion, and opportunity to dress up and shmooze – no, that's unnecessary, nasty, yes it is – let's rather say they try to support each other – in life and especially in death. When they're not too busy bitching, and gossiping about each other.

Milton. He's been looking at all the photos my cousin Mae has put up on a board beside the corpse, my corpse, and fucking embarrassing most of them are. But worth a passing smile. Me as a baby, me in my new suit for confirmation, me flying my kite, me at Mae's wedding – I remember that cute blond American, how we went at it in the washroom, he had a plane to catch, I wonder what happened to him? Who was he?

But you were so cute too, Milton. I remember when we met, at that DQ show in TO, Hart House Theater – all those Queens! I was there to pick up some tips, of course, for my own act back at the Werx – but here you were, so beautiful, baby, your big blue eyes, film-star profile, and sitting right beside me, laughing and clapping, so unselfconscious, Mister Enthusiasm! – I couldn't believe you were on your own, but you were. And, as it all ended, you turned to me and said "Wasn't that great?" and I agreed Yes, yes, yes – and then we stood outside and talked, how and why it was such a fabulous show – "kinda sad" you said, because it was the final one, end of the line, they said, and a memorial to the great June Callwood, she started it, raising money for an AIDS hospice, and now she was gone – "but also it's kinda happy", with all those Queens in their fabulous costumes singing and prancing, "having such a ball, giving themselves and us so much joy". And I knew we'd get it on, and I kissed you, long and hard – you were so hot -

Yes, but that was then, and now is now, and it's almost gone. So, Milton, baby, pay attention! I want you to sit in that seat beside Terry – Yes, that older man in the dark blue suit, that's the one – he's looking at you, recognizing you – No, *you* don't recognize *him*, of course you don't, he's a stranger to you, I never even mentioned Terry to you, and you wouldn't have been interested anyway, would you? But of course Terry, masochistic Terry, wanted to see *you*, and I noticed him at least once watching you and me in the Werx. When I'd finished my Marilyn Monroe number and, surrounded by admirers, was quenching my urgent thirst. For beer, on that occasion, baby – don't try to be clever, doesn't suit you.

Milton! Hey, don't you go past him, don't glance at him so casually, don't give him the look that young gays give older ones, the look that says "Buddy, you don't fucking *exist* for me." Oh Milton! Was it because I didn't focus my message enough, didn't you hear what I said? Ah, but there you are, you *did* hear me after all. And you actually exchange a semi-smile with Terry, the kind of sad smirk that may be considered appropriate in this setting. Maybe he's wondering why you chose to sit beside him – I hope so. Yes, I can feel his interest modulating into that preliminary sexual quiver of the shrouded penis – oh how I'll miss that! You haven't lost your charisma, have you, baby?

Now pay attention, both of you. The stage is set, the curtain is rising. Music, maestro! Actually there's been music all along, of the organ-muzack kind, a kinda holy groan. But now there'll be a hymn or two, giving a mournful jollity to boring proceedings that I think I'll be fortunate to miss, if I do. I wonder who's in charge here? – Oh, there he is, a plump, gowned, pompous-looking minister, another

Queen, contributed by Milton's Church, for a largish sum no doubt, and at this moment checking his radiantly empathetic smile in a convenient mirror. He'll march forth any minute. Onward, Christian soldier! If I am to remain and observe, please let him be brief -

But now I feel coldness spreading fast and faster through my airy bones. The scene is drenched in grey – I can't discern those two at all clearly now. But they are there, I know they are, my Terry and my Milton, sitting together, perhaps holding hands by now? I give you to each other, darlings. A reward for all the suffering I caused you. I am confident that, in loving tribute to me, the Deceased – the silent centre of this show, a star at last! – the one who has so suddenly dropped out of your lives, courtesy of that fucking speeding car – I am confident that you will ripen your connection into companionship, and then by increasingly rapid stages reach the lust that will whirl you onward to your destination – Love? Love each other while you can, my dears.

And *I* am ready for *my* destination, wherever or whatever it is. Oh, black, black! Here I go! Wow! LOL, guys – and watch out, you two, for speeding cars.

Yes, yes. *Yes.*